Traffic in S

A Novel of Crime and Its Cure

Eustace Hale Ball

Alpha Editions

This edition published in 2024

ISBN : 9789357967457

Design and Setting By
Alpha Editions
www.alphaedis.com
Email - info@alphaedis.com

As per information held with us this book is in Public Domain.
This book is a reproduction of an important historical work. Alpha Editions uses the best technology to reproduce historical work in the same manner it was first published to preserve its original nature. Any marks or number seen are left intentionally to preserve its true form.

Contents

CHAPTER I ....- 1 -
CHAPTER II ....- 15 -
CHAPTER III ....- 22 -
CHAPTER IV ....- 31 -
CHAPTER V ....- 42 -
CHAPTER VI ....- 49 -
CHAPTER VII ....- 60 -
CHAPTER VIII ....- 70 -
CHAPTER IX ....- 77 -
CHAPTER X ....- 89 -
CHAPTER XI ....- 94 -
CHAPTER XII ....- 102 -
CHAPTER XIII ....- 115 -
CHAPTER XIV ....- 123 -
CHAPTER XV ....- 136 -

CHAPTER I

NIGHT COURT

Officer 4434 beat his freezing hands together as he stood with his back to the snow-laden north-easter, which rattled the creaking signboards of East Twelfth Street, and covered, with its merciful shroud of wet flakes, the ash-barrels, dingy stoops, gaudy saloon porticos and other architectural beauties of the Avenue corner.

Officer 4434 was on "fixed post."

This is an institution of the New York police department which makes it possible for citizens to locate, in time of need, a representative of the law. At certain street crossings throughout the boroughs bluecoats are assigned to guard-duty during the night, where they can keep close watch on the neighboring thoroughfares. The "fixed post" increases the efficiency of the service, but it is a bitter ordeal on the men.

Officer 4434 shivered under his great coat. He pulled the storm hood of his cap closer about his neck as he muttered an opinion, far from being as cold as the biting blast, concerning the Commissioner who had installed the system. He had been on duty over an hour, and even his sturdy young physique was beginning to feel the strain of the Arctic temperature.

"I wonder when Maguire is coming to relieve me?" muttered 4434, when suddenly his mind left the subject, as his keen vision descried two struggling figures a few yards down the dark side of Twelfth Street.

There was no outcry for help. But 4434 knew his precinct too well to wait for that. He quietly walked to the left corner and down toward the couple. As he neared them the mist of the eddying snowflakes became less dense; he could discern a short man twisting the arm of a tall woman, who seemed to be top heavy from an enormous black-plumed hat. The faces of the twain were still indistinct. The man whirled the woman about roughly. She uttered a subdued moan of pain, and 4434, as he softly approached them, his footfalls muffled by the blanket of white, could hear her pleading in a low tone with the man.

"Aw, kid, I ain't got none ... I swear I ain't... Oh, oh ... ye know I wouldn't lie to ye, kid!"

"Nix, Annie. Out wid it, er I'll bust yer damn arm!"

"Jimmie, I ain't raised a nickel to-night ... dere ain't even a sailor out a night like dis... Oh, oh, kid, don't treat me dis way..."

Her voice died down to a gasp of pain.

Officer 4434 was within ten feet of the couple by this time. He recognized the type though not the features of the man, who had now wrenched the woman's arm behind her so cruelly that she had fallen to her knees, in the snow. The fellow was so intent upon his quest for money that he did not observe the approach of the policeman.

But the woman caught a quick glimpse of the intruder into their "domestic" affairs. She tried to warn her companion.

"Jimmie, dere's a..."

She did not finish, for her companion wished to end further argument with his own particular repartee.

He swung viciously with his left arm and brought a hard fist across the woman's pleading lips. She screamed and sank back limply.

As she did so, Officer 4434 reached forward with a vise-like grip and closed his tense fingers about the back of Jimmie's muscular neck. Holding his night stick in readiness for trouble, with that knack peculiar to policemen, he yanked the tough backward and threw him to his knees. Annie sprang to her feet.

"Lemme go!" gurgled the surprised Jimmie, as he wriggled to get free. Without a word, the woman who had been suffering from his brutality, now sprang upon the rescuing policeman with the fury of a lioness robbed of her cub. She clawed at the bluecoat's face and cursed him with volubility.

"I'll git you broke fer this!" groaned Jimmie, as 4434 held him to his knees, while Annie tried to get her hold on the officer's neck. It was a temptation to swing the night-stick, according to the laws of war, and then protect himself against the fury of the frenzied woman. But, this is an impulse which the policeman is trained to subdue—public opinion on the subject to the contrary notwithstanding. Officer 4434 knew the influence of the gangsters with certain politicians, who had influence with the magistrates, who in turn meted out summary reprimands and penalties to policemen un-Spartanlike enough to defend themselves with their legal weapons against the henchmen of the East Side politicians!

Annie had managed by no mean pugilistic ability to criss-cross five painful scratches with her nails, upon the policeman's face, despite his attempt to guard himself.

Jimmie, with tactical resourcefulness, had twisted around in such a way that he delivered a strong-jaw nip on the right leg of the policeman.

4434 suddenly released his hold on the man's neck, whipped out his revolver and fired it in the air. He would have used the signal for help generally available at such a time, striking the night stick upon the pavement, but the thick snow would have muffled the resonant alarm.

"Beat it, Annie, and git de gang!" cried out Jimmie as he scrambled to his feet. The woman sped away obediently, as Officer 4434 closed in again upon his prisoner. The gangster covered the retreat of the woman by grappling the policeman with arms and legs.

The two fell to the pavement, and writhed in their struggle on the snow.

Jimmie, like many of the gang men, was a local pugilist of no mean ability. His short stature was equalized in fighting odds by a tremendous bull strength. 4434, in his heavy overcoat, and with the storm hood over his head and neck was somewhat handicapped. Even as they struggled, the efforts of the nimble Annie bore fruit. In surprisingly brief time a dozen men had rushed out from the neighboring saloon, and were giving the doughty policeman more trouble than he could handle.

Suddenly they ran, however, for down the street came two speeding figures in the familiar blue coats. One of the officers was shrilly blowing his whistle for reinforcements. He knew what to expect in a gang battle and was taking no chances.

Maguire, who had just come on to relieve 4434, lived up to his duty most practically by catching the leg of the battling Jimmie, and giving it a wrestling twist which threw the tough with a thud on the pavement, clear of his antagonist.

4434 rose to his feet stiffly, as his rescuers dragged Jimmie to a standing position.

"Well, Burke, 'tis a pleasant little party you do be having," volunteered Maguire. "Sure, and you've been rassling with Jimmie the Monk. Was he trying to pick yer pockets?"

"Naw, I wasn't doin' nawthin', an' I'm goin' ter git that rookie broke fer assaultin' me. I'm goin' ter write a letter to the Mayor!" growled Jimmie.

Officer Burke laughed a bit ruefully.

He mopped some blood off his face, from the nail scratches of Jimmie's lady associate, and then turned toward the two officers.

"He didn't pick my pockets—it was just the old story, of beating up his woman, trying to get the money she made on the street to-night. When I tried to help her they both turned on me."

"Faith, Burke, I thought you had more horse sense," responded Maguire. "That's a dangerous thing to do with married folks, or them as ought to be married. They'll fight like Kilkenny cats until the good Samaritan comes along and then they form a trust and beat up the Samaritan."

"I think most women these days need a little beating up anyway, to keep 'em from worrying about their troubles," volunteered Officer Dexter. "I'd have been happier if I had learned that in time."

"Say, nix on dis blarney, youse!" interrupted the Monk, who was trying to wriggle out of the arm hold of Burke and Maguire. "I ain't gonter stand fer dis pinch wen I ain't done nawthin."

A police sergeant, who had heard the whistle as he made his rounds, now came up.

"What's the row?" he gruffly exclaimed. Burke explained. The sergeant shook his head.

"You're wasting time, Burke, on this sort of stuff. When you've been on the force a while longer you'll learn that it's the easiest thing to look the other way when you see these men fighting with their women. The magistrates won't do a thing on a policeman's word alone. You just see. Now you've got to go down to Night Court with this man, get a call down because you haven't got a witness, and this rummie gets set free. Why, you'd think these magistrates had to apologize for there being a police force! The papers go on about the brutality of the police, and the socialists howl about Cossack methods, and the ministers preach about graft and vice, and the reformers sit in their mahogany chairs in the skyscraper offices and dictate poems about sin, and the cops have to walk around and get hell beat out of 'em by these wops and kikes every time they tries to keep a little order!"

The sergeant turned to Maguire.

"You know these gangs around here, Mack. Who's this guy's girl?"

"He's got three or four, sergeant," responded the officer. "I guess this one must be Dutch Annie. Was she all dolled up with about a hundred dollars' worth of ostrich feathers, Burke?"

"Yes—tall, and some fighter."

"That's the one. Her hangout is over there on the corner, in Shultberger's cabaret. We can get her now, maybe."

The sergeant beckoned to Dexter.

"Run this guy over to the station house, and put him down on the blotter for disorderly conduct, and assaulting an officer. You get onto your post,

Maguire, or the Commish'll be shooting past here in a machine on the way to some ball at the Ritz, and will have us all on charges. You come with me, Burke, and we'll nab that woman as a material witness."

Burke and his superior crossed the street and quickly entered the ornate portal of Shultberger's cabaret, which was in reality the annex to his corner barroom.

As they strode in a waiter stood by a tuneless piano, upon which a bloated "professor" was beating a tattoo of cheap syncopation accompaniment of the advantages of "Bobbin' Up An' Down," which was warbled with that peculiarly raucous, nasal tenor so popular in Tenderloin resorts. The musical waiter's jaw fell in the middle of a bob, as he espied the blue uniforms.

He disappeared behind a swinging door with the professional skill of a stage magician.

Sitting around the dilapidated wooden tables was a motley throng of red-nosed women, loafers, heavy-jowled young aliens, and a scattering of young girls attired in cheap finery; a prevailing color of chemical yellow as to hair, and flaming red cheeks and lips.

Instinctively the gathering rose for escape, but the sergeant strode forward to one particular table, where sat a girl nursing a bleeding mouth.

Burke remained by the door to shut off that exit.

"Is this the one?" asked the sergeant, as he put his hands on the young woman's shoulder.

Burke scrutinized her closely, responding quickly.

"Yes!"

"Come on, you," ordered the roundsman. "I want you. Quick!"

"Say, I ain't done a thing, what do ye want me fer?" whined the girl, as the sergeant pulled at her sleeve. The officer did not reply, but he looked menacingly about him at the evil company.

"If any of you guys starts anything I'm going to call out the reserves. Come on, Annie."

The proprietor, Shultberger, now entered from the front, after a warning from his waiter.

"Vot's dis, sergeant? Vot you buttin' in my place for? Ain't I in right?" he cried.

"Shut up. This girl has been assaulting an officer, and I want her. Come on, now, or I'll get the wagon here, and then there will be trouble."

Annie began to pull back, and it looked as though some of the toughs would interfere. But Shultberger understood his business.

"Now, Annie, don't start nottings here. Go on vid de officer. I'll fix it up all right. But I don't vant my place down on de blotter. Who vas it—Jimmie?"

The girl began to cry, and gulped the glass of whiskey on the table as she finally yielded to the tug of the sergeant.

"Yes, it's Jimmie. An' he wasn't doin' a ting. Dese rookies is always makin' trouble fer me."

She sobbed hysterically as the sergeant walked her out. Shultberger patted her on the shoulder reassuringly.

"Dot's all right, Annie. I vouldn't let nodding happen to Jimmie. I'll bail him out and you too. Go along; dot's a good girl." He turned to his guests, and motioned to them to be silent.

The "professor," at the piano, used to such scenes, lulled the nerves of the company with a rag-time variation of "Oh, You Beautiful Doll," and Burke, the sergeant and Annie went out into the night.

The girl was taken to the station. The lieutenant looked questioningly at Officer 4434.

"Want to put her down for assault?" he asked.

Burke looked at the unhappy creature. Her hair was half-down her back, and her lips swollen and bleeding from Jimmie's brutal blow. The cheap rouge on her face; the heavy pencilling of her brows, the crudely applied blue and black grease paint about her eyes, the tawdry paste necklace around her powdered throat; the pitifully thin silk dress in which she had braved the elements for a few miserable dollars: all these brought tears to the eyes of the young officer.

He was sick at heart.

The girl shivered and sobbed in that hysterical manner which indicates weakness, emptiness, lack of soul—rather than sorrow.

"Poor thing—I couldn't do it. I don't want to see her sent to Blackwell's Island. She's getting enough punishment every day—and every night."

"Well, she's made your face look like a railroad map. You're too soft, young fellow. I'll put her down as a material witness. Go wash that blood off, and we'll send 'em both down to Night Court. You've done yourself out of your relief butting in this way. Take a tip from me, and let these rummies fight it out among themselves after this as long as they don't mix up with somebody worth while."

Burke wiped his eye with the back of his cold hand. It was not snow which had melted there. He was young enough in the police service to feel the pathos of even such common situations as this.

He turned quietly and went back to the washstand in the rear room of the station. The reserves were sitting about, playing checkers and cards. Some were reading.

Half a dozen of the men, fond of the young policeman, chatted with him, and volunteered advice, to which Burke had no reply.

"Don't start in mixing up with the Gas Tank Gang over one of those girls, Burke, for they're not worth it."

"You'll have enough to do in this precinct to look after your own skin, and round up the street holdups, or get singed at a tenement fire."

And so it went.

The worldly wisdom of his fellows was far from encouraging. Yet, despite their cynical expressions, Burke knew that warm hearts and gallant chivalry were lodged beneath the brass buttons.

There is a current notion among the millions of Americans who do not know, and who have fortunately for themselves not been in the position where they needed to know, that the policemen of New York are an organized body of tyrannical, lying grafters who maintain their power by secret societies, official connivance and criminal brute force.

Taken by and large, there is no fighting organization in any army in the world which can compare with the New York police force for physical equipment, quick action under orders or upon the initiative required by emergencies, gallantry or *esprit de corps*. For salaries barely equal to those of poorly paid clerks or teamsters, these men risk their lives daily, must face death at any moment, and are held under a discipline no less rigorous than that of the regular army. Their problems are more complex than those of any soldiery; they deal with fifty different nationalities, and are forced by circumstances to act as judge and jury, as firemen, as life savers, as directories, as arbiters of neighborhood squabbles and domestic wrangles. Their greatest services are rendered in the majority of cases which never call for arrest and prosecution. That there are many instances of petty "graft," and that, in some cases, the "middle men" prey on the underworld cannot be denied.

But it is the case against a certain policeman which receives the attention of the newspapers and the condemnation of the public, while almost unheeded are scores of heroic deeds which receive bare mention in the daily press. For the misdeed of one bad policeman the gallantry and self-sacrifice of a hundred pass without appreciation.

There have been but three recorded instances of cowardice in the annals of the New York police force. The memory of them still rankles in the bosom of every member. And yet the performance of duty at the cost of life and limb is regarded by the uniformed men as merely being "all in the day's work." The men are anxious to do their duty in every way, but political, religious, social and commercial influences are continually erecting stone walls across the path of that duty.

Superhuman in wisdom, thrice blest in luck is the bluecoat who conscientiously can live up to his own ideals, carry out the law as written by his superiors without being sent to "rusticate with the goats," or being demoted for stepping upon the toes of some of those same superiors!

Officer Bobbie Burke betook himself to the Night Court to lodge his complaint against Jimmie the Monk. The woman, Dutch Annie, sniveling and sobbing, was lodged in a cell near the gangster before being brought before the rail to face the magistrate.

Burke saw that they could not communicate with each other, and so hoped that he could have his own story accepted by the magistrate. He stood by the door of the crowded detention room, which opened into a larger courtroom, where the prisoners were led one by one to the prisoner's dock—in this case, a hand-rail two feet in front of the long desk of the judge, while that worthy was seated on a platform which enabled him to look down at the faces of the arraigned.

It was an apparently endless procession.

The class of arrests was monotonous. Three of every four cases were those of street women who had been arrested by "plain clothes" men or detectives for solicitation on the street.

The accusing officer took a chair at the left of the magistrate. The uniformed attendant handed the magistrate the affidavits of complaint. The judge mechanically scrawled his name at the bottom of the papers, glanced at the words of the arraignments, and then scowled over the edge of his desk at the flashily dressed girls before him. They all seemed slight variations on the same mould.

Perhaps one girl would simulate some hysterical sobs, and begin by protesting her innocence. Another would be hard and indifferent. A third, indignant.

"What about this, officer?" the judge would ask. "Where did you see this woman, what did you say, what did she say, and what happened?"

The detective, in a voice and manner as mechanical as that of the judge, would mumble his oft repeated story, giving the exact minute of his observations, the actions of the woman in accosting different pedestrians and in her final approach to him.

"How many times before have you been arrested, girl?" the magistrate would growl.

Sometimes the girls would admit the times; in most cases their memories were defective, until the accusing officer would cite past history. This girl had been arrested and paroled once before; that one had been sent to "the Island" for thirty days; the next one was an habitual offender. It was a tragic monotony. Sometimes the magistrate would summon the sweet-faced matron to have a talk with some young girl, evidently a "green one" for whom there might be hope. There was more kindliness and effort to reform the prisoners behind those piercing eyes of the judge than one might have supposed to hear him drone out his judgment: "Thirty days, Molly"; "Ten dollars, Aggie—the Island next time, sure"; "Five dollars for you, Sadie," and so on. There was a weary, hopeless look in the magistrate's eyes, had you studied him close at hand. He knew, better than the reformers, of the horrors of the social evil, at the very bottom of the cup of sin. Better than they could he understand the futility of garrulous legislation at the State Capitol, to be offset by ignorance, avarice, weakness and disease in the congestion of the big, unwieldy city. When he fined the girls he knew that it meant only a hungry day, one less silk garment or perhaps a beating from an angry and disappointed "lover." When he sent them to the workhouse their activities were merely discontinued for a while to learn more vileness from companions in their imprisonment; to make for greater industry—busier vice and quicker disease upon their return to the streets. The occasional cases in which there was some chance for regeneration were more welcome to him, even, than to the weak and sobbing girls, hopeless with the misery of their early defeats. Yet, the magistrate knew only too well the miserable minimum of cases which ever resulted in real rescue and removal from the sordid existence.

Once as low as the rail of the Night Court—a girl seldom escaped from the slime into which she had dragged herself. And yet *had* she dragged herself there? Was *she* to blame? Was she to pay the consequences in the last Reckoning of Accounts?

This thought came to Officer Bobbie Burke as he watched the horrible drama drag monotonously through its brief succession of sordid scenes.

The expression of the magistrate, the same look of sympathetic misery on the face of the matron, and even on many of the detectives, automatons who had chanted this same official requiem of dead souls, years of nights ... not a sombre tone of the gruesome picture was lost to Burke's keen eyes.

"Some one has to pay; some one has to pay! I wonder who?" muttered Officer 4434 under his breath.

There were cases of a different caliber. Yet Burke could see in them what Balzac called "social coördination."

Now a middle-aged woman, with hair unkempt, and hat awry, maudlin tears in her swollen eyes, and swaying as she held the rail, looked shiftily up into the magistrate's immobile face.

"You've been drunk again, Mrs. Rafferty? This is twice during the last fortnight that I've had you here."

"Yis, yer honor, an me wid two foine girls left home. Oh, Saint Mary protect me, an' oi'm a (hic) bad woman. Yer honor, it's the fault of me old man, Pat. (Hic) Oi'm *not* a bad woman, yer honor."

The magistrate was kind as he spoke.

"And what does Pat do?"

"He beats me, yer honor (hic), until Oi sneak out to the family intrance at the corner fer a quiet nip ter fergit it. An' the girls, they've been supportin' me (hic), an' payin the rint, an' buyin' the vittles, an' (hic) it's a dog's life they lead, wid all their work. When they go out wid dacint young min (hic), Pat cusses the young min, an' beats the girls whin they come home (hic)."

Here the woman broke down, sobbing, while the attendant kept her from swaying and falling.

"There, there, Mrs. Rafferty. I'll suspend sentence this time. But don't let it happen another time. You have Pat arrested and I'll teach him something about treating you right."

"My God, yer honor (hic), the worst of it is it's me two girls—they ain't got no home, but a drunken din, the next thing I knows they'll be arrested (hic) and brought up before ye like these other poor divvels. Yer honor, it's drunken Pats and min like him that's bringin' these poor girls here—it ain't the cops an' the sports (hic), yer honor."

The woman staggered as the magistrate quietly signaled the attendant to lead her through the gate, and up the aisle of the court to the outer door.

As she passed by the spectators, two or three richly dressed young women giggled and nudged the dapper youths with whom they were sitting.

"Silence!" cried the magistrate tersely. "This is not a cabaret show. I don't want any seeing-New-York parties here. Sergeant, put those people out of the court."

The officer walked up the aisle and ordered the society buds and their escorts to leave.

"Why, we're studying sociology," murmured one girl. "It's a very stupid thing, however, down here."

"So vulgar, my dear," acquiesced her friend. "There's nothing interesting anyway. Just the same old story."

They noisily arose, and walked out, while Officer Burke could hear one of the gilded youths exclaim in a loud voice as they reached the outer corridor:

"Come on, let's go up to Rector's for a little tango, and see some real life...."

The magistrate who had heard it tapped his pen on the desk, and looked quizzically at the matron.

"They are doubtless preparing some reform legislation for the suffrage platform, Mrs. Grey, and I have inadvertently delayed the millennium. Ah, a pity!"

Burke was impatient for the calling of his own case. He was tired. He would have been hungry had he not been so nauseated by the sickening environment. He longed for the fresh air; even the snowstorm was better than this.

But his turn had not come. The next to be called was another answer to his mental question.

A young woman with a blackened eye and a bleeding cheek was brought in by a fat, jolly officer, who led a burly, sodden man with him.

The charge was quarreling and destroying the furniture of a neighbor in whose flat the fight had taken place.

"Who started it?" asked the magistrate.

"She did, your honor. She ain't never home when I wants my vittles cooked, and she blows my money so there ain't nothing in the house to eat for meself. She's always startin' things, and she did this time when I tells her to come on home...."

"Just a minute," interrupted the magistrate. "What is the cause of this, little woman? Who struck you on the eye?"

The woman's lips trembled, and she glanced at the big fellow beside her. He glowered down at her with a threatening twist of his mouth.

"Why, your honor, you see, the baby was sick, and Joe, he went out with the boys pay night, and we didn't have a cent in the flat, and I had to..."

"Shut up, or I'll bust you when I get you alone!" muttered Joe, until the judge pounded on the table with his gavel.

"You won't be where you can bust her!" sharply exclaimed the magistrate. "Go on, little woman. When did he hit you?"

The wife trembled and hesitated. The magistrate nodded encouragingly.

"Why weren't you home?" he asked softly.

"My neighbor, Mrs. Goldberg, likes the baby, and she was showing me how to make some syrup for its croup, your honor, sir. We haven't got any light—it's a quarter gas meter, and there wasn't anything to cook with, and I had the baby in her flat, and Joe he just got home—he hadn't been there ... since ... Saturday night ... I didn't have anything to eat—since then, myself."

Joe whirled about threateningly, but the officer caught his uplifted arm.

"She lies. She ain't straight, that's what it is. Hanging around them *Sheenies*, and sayin' it's the baby. She lies!"

The little woman's face paled, and she staggered back, her tremulous fingers clutching at the empty air as her great eyes opened with horror at his words.

"I'm not *straight*? Oh, oh, Joe! You're killing me!"

She moaned as though the man had beat her again.

"Six months!" rasped out the magistrate between his teeth. "And I'm going to put you under a peace bond when you get out. Little woman, you're dismissed."

Joe was roughly jostled out into the detention room again by the rosy-cheeked policeman, whose face was neither so jolly nor rosy now. The woman sobbed, and leaned across the rail, her outstretched arms held pleadingly toward the magistrate.

"Oh, judge, sir ... don't send him up for six months. How can the baby and I live? We have no one, not one soul to care for us, and I'm expecting..."

Mercifully her nerves gave way, and she fainted. The gruff old court attendant, now as gentle as a nurse, caught her, and with the gateman, carried her at the judge's direction, toward his own private office, whither hurried Mrs. Grey, the matron.

The magistrate blew his nose, rubbed his glasses, and irritably looked at the next paper.

"Jimmie Olinski. Officer Burke. Hurry up, I want to call recess!" he exclaimed.

Burke, in a daze of thoughts, pulled himself together, and then took the arm of Jimmie the Monk, who advanced with manner docile and obsequious. He was not a stranger to the path to the rail. Another officer led Annie forward. Burke took the chair.

"Don't waste my time," snapped the magistrate. "What's this? Another fight?"

Officer 4434 explained the situation.

"Do you want to complain, woman?" asked the magistrate.

"Complain, why yer honor, dis cop is lyin' like a house afire. Dis is me gent' friend, an' I got me face hoit by dis cop hittin' me when he butted into our conversation. Dis cop assaulted us both, yer honor."

"That'll do. Shut up. You know what this is, don't you, Burke? The same old story. Why do you waste time on this sort of thing unless you've got a witness? You know one of these women will never testify against the man, no matter how much he beats and robs her."

"But, your honor, the man assaulted her and assaulted me," began Burke.

"She doesn't count. That's the pity of it, poor thing. I'll hold him over to General Sessions for a criminal trial on assaulting you."

In the back of the room a stout man in a fur overcoat arose.

It was Shultberger. He came down the aisle.

As he did so, unnoticed by Officer 4434, three of Shultberger's companions arose and quietly left the courtroom by the front entrance.

"Oxcuse me, Chudge, but may I offer bail for my friend, little Jimmie?"

He had some papers in his hand, for this was what might be called a by-product of his saloon business; Shultberger was always ready for the assistance of his clients.

The magistrate looked sharply at him. "Down here again, eh? I'd think those deeds and that old brick house would be worn out by this time, Shultberger, from the frequency with which you juggle it against the liberty of your friends."

"It's a fine house, Chudge, and was assessed."

"Yes—go file your papers," snapped the magistrate. "You can report back to your station house, officer. There is no charge against this girl—she is merely held as material witness. She'll never testify. She's discharged. Take my advice, Burke, and play safe with these gun-men. You're in a neighborhood which needs good precaution as well as good intentions. Good night."

The magistrate rose, declaring a recess for one hour, and Officer 4434 left the court through the police entrance.

As he turned the corner of the old Court building, he repeated to himself the question which had forced itself so strongly upon him: "Who is to blame? Who has to pay? The men or the women?"

Again he saw, mentally, the sobbing, drunken Irish woman with the two daughters who had no home life. He saw the brutal Joe, and his fainting wife as he cast the horrible words "not straight" into her soul. He saw that the answer to his question, and the shallow society youngsters, who had left the courtroom to see "real life" at Rector's, were not disconnected from that answer.

But he did not see a dark form behind a stone buttress at the corner of the old building. He did not see a brick which came hurtling through the air from behind him.

He merely fell forward, mutely—with a fractured skull!

CHAPTER II

WHEN LOVE COMES VISITING

It was a very weak young man who sojourned for the next few weeks in the hospital, hovering so near the shadow of the Eternal Fixed Post that nurses and internes gave him up many times.

"It's only his fine young body, with a fine clean mind and fine living behind it, that has brought him around, nurse," said Doctor MacFarland, the police surgeon of Burke's precinct, as he came to make his daily call.

"He's been very patient, sir, and it's a blessing to see him able to sit up now, and take an interest in things. Many a man's mind has been a blank after such a blow and such a fracture. He's a great favorite, here," said the pretty nurse.

Old Doctor MacFarland gave her a comical wink as he answered.

"Well, nurse, beware of these great favorites. I like him myself, and every officer on the force who knows him does as well. But the life of a policeman's wife is not quite as jolly and rollicking as that of a grateful patient who happens to be a millionaire. So, bide your time."

He chuckled and walked on down the hall, while the young woman blushed a carmine which made her look very pretty as she entered the private room which had been reserved for Bobbie Burke.

"Is there anything you would like for a change?" she asked.

"Well, I can't read, and I can't take up all your time talking, so I wish you'd let me get out of this room into one of the wards in a wheel-chair, nurse," answered Burke. "I'd like to see some of the other folks, if it's permissible."

"That's easy. The doctor said you could sit up more each day now. He says you'll be back on duty in another three weeks—or maybe six."

Burke groaned.

"Oh, these doctors, really, I feel as well now as I ever did, except that my head is just a little wobbly and I don't believe I could beat Longboat in a Marathon. But, you see, I'll be back on duty before any three weeks go by."

Burke was wheeled out into the big free ward of the hospital by one of the attendants. He had never realized how much human misery could be concentrated into one room until that perambulatory trip.

It was not a visiting day, and many of the sufferers tossed about restless and unhappy.

About some of the beds there were screens—to keep the sight of their unhappiness and anguish from their neighbors.

Here was a man whose leg had been amputated. His entire life was blighted because he had stuck to his job, coupling freight cars, when the engineer lost his head.

There, on that bed, was an old man who had saved a dozen youngsters from a burning Christmas tree, and was now paying the penalty with months of torture.

Yonder poor fellow, braving the odds of the city, had left his country town, sought labor vainly, until he was found starving rather than beg.

As a policeman, Burke had seen many miseries in his short experience on the force; as an invalid he had been initiated into the second degree in this hospital ward. He wondered if there could be anything more bitter. There was—his third and final degree in the ritual of life: but that comes later on in our story.

After chatting here and there with a sufferer, passing a friendly word of encouragement, or spinning some droll old yarn to cheer up another, Bobbie had enough.

"Say, it's warm looking outside. Could I get some fresh air on one of the sun-porches?" he asked his steersman.

"Sure thing, cap. I'll blanket you up a bit, and put you through your paces on the south porch."

Bobbie was rolled out on the glass protected porch into the blessed rays of the sun. He found another traveler using the same mode of conveyance, an elderly man, whose pallid face, seamed with lines of suffering, still showed the jolly, unconquerable spirit which keeps some men young no matter how old they grow.

"Well, it's about the finest sunlight I've seen for many a day. How do you like it, young man?"

"It's the first I've had for so many weeks that I didn't believe there was any left in the world," responded Burke. "If we could only get out for a walk instead of this Atlantic City boardwalk business it would be better, wouldn't it?"

His companion nodded, but his genial smile vanished.

"Yes, but that's something I'll never get again."

"What, never again? Why, surely you're getting along to have them bring you out here?"

"No, my boy. I've a broken hip, and a broken thigh. Crushed in an elevator accident, back in the factory, and I'm too old a dog to learn to do such tricks as flying. I'll have to content myself with one of these chairs for the rest of my worthless old years."

The old man sighed, and such a sigh!

Bobbie's heart went out to him, and he tried to cheer him up.

"Well, sir, there could be worse things in life—you are not blind, nor deaf—you have your hands and they look like hands that can do a lot."

His neighbor looked down at his nervous, delicate hands and smiled, for his was a valiant spirit.

"Yes, they've done a lot. They'll do a lot more, for I've been lying on my back with nothing to do for a month but think up things for them to do. I'm a mechanic, you know, and fortunately I have my hands and my memory, and years of training. I've been superintendent of a factory; electrical work, phonographs, and all kinds of instruments like that were my specialty. But, they don't want an old man back there, now. Too many young bloods with college training and book knowledge. I couldn't superintend much work now—this wheel chair of mine is built for comfort rather than exceeding the speed limit."

Burke drew him out, and learned another pitiful side of life.

Burke's new acquaintance was an artisan of the old school, albeit with the skill and modernity of a man who keeps himself constantly in the forefront by youthful thinking and scientific work. He had devoted the best years of his life to the interests of his employer. When a splendid factory had been completed, largely through the results of his executive as well as his technical skill, and an enormous fortune accumulated from the growing business of the famous plant, the president of the company had died. His son, fresh from college, assumed the management of the organization, and the services of old Barton were little appreciated by the younger man or his board of directors. It was a familiar story of modern business life.

"So, there you have it, young man. Why I should bother you with my troubles I don't quite understand myself. In a hospital it's like shipboard; we know a man a short while, and isolated from the rest of the world, we are drawn closer than with the acquaintances of years. In my case it's just the tragedy of age. There is no man so important but that a business goes on very well without him. I realized it with young Gresham, even before I was hurt in the factory. They had taken practically all I had to give, and it was time to cast me aside. As a sort of charity, Gresham has sent me four weeks' salary, with a letter saying that he can do no more, and has appointed a young electrical engineer, from his own class in Yale, to take my place. They need an active man, not an invalid. My salary has been used up for expenses, and for the living of my two daughters, Mary and Lorna. What I'll do when I get back home, I don't know."

He shook his head, striving to conceal the despondency which was tugging at his heart.

Burke was cheery as he responded.

"Well, Mr. Barton, you're not out of date yet. The world of electricity is getting bigger every day. You say that you have made many patents which were given to the Gresham company because you were their employee. Now, you can turn out a few more with your own name on them, and get the profits yourself. That's not so bad. I'll be out of here myself, before long, and I'll stir myself, to see that you get a chance. I can perhaps help in some way, even if I'm only a policeman."

The older man looked at him with a comical surprise.

"A policeman? A cop? Well, well, well! I wouldn't have known it!"

Bobbie Burke laughed, and he had a merry laugh that did one's soul good to hear.

"We're just human beings, you know—even if the ministers and the muckrakers do accuse us of being blood brothers to the devil and Ali Baba."

"I never saw a policeman out of uniform before—that's why it seems funny, I suppose. But I wouldn't judge you to be the type which I usually see in the police. How long have you been in the service?"

Here was Bobby's cue for autobiography, and he realized that, as a matter of neighborliness, he must go as far as his friend.

"Well, I'm what they call a rookie. It's my second job as a rookie, however, for I ran away from home several years ago, and joined the army. I believed all the pretty pictures they hang up in barber shops and country post-offices, and thought I was going to be a globe trotter. Do you remember that masterpiece which shows the gallant bugler tooting the 'Blue Bells of Scotland,' and wearing a straight front jacket that would make a Paris dressmaker green with envy? Well, sir, I believed that poster, and the result was that I went to the Philippines and helped chase Malays, Filipinos, mosquitoes, and germs; curried the major's horse, swept his front porch, polished his shoes, built fences and chicken houses, and all the rest of the things a soldier does."

"But, why didn't you stay at home?"

Burke dropped his eyes for an instant, and then looked up unhappily.

"I had no real home. My mother and father died the same year, when I was eighteen. I don't know how it all happened. I had gone to college out West for one year, when my uncle sent for me to come back to the town where we lived and get to work. My father was rather well to do, and I couldn't quite understand it. But, my uncle was executor of the estate, and when I had been away that season it was all done. There was no estate when I got back, and there was nothing to do but to work for my uncle in the store which he said he had bought from my father, and to live up in the little room on the third floor where the cook used to sleep, in the house where I was born, which he said he had bought from the estate. It was a queer game. My father left no records of a lot of things, and so there you know why I ran away to listen to that picture bugle. I re-enlisted, and at the end of my second service I got sick of it. I was a sergeant and was going to take the examination for second lieutenant when I got malaria, and I decided that the States were good enough for me. The Colonel knew the Police Commissioner here. He sent me a rattling good letter. I never expected to use it. But, after I hunted a job for six months and spent every cent I had, I decided that soldiering was a good training for sweeping front porches and polishing rifles, but it didn't pay much gas and rent in the big city. The soldier is a baby who always takes orders from dad, and dad is the government. I decided I'd use what training I had, so I took that letter to the Commissioner. I got through the examinations, and landed on the force. Then a brick with a nice sharp corner landed on the back of my head, and I landed up here. And that's all there is to *my* tale of woe."

The old man looked at him genially.

"Well, you've had your own hard times, my boy. None of us finds it all as pretty as the picture of the bugler, whether we work in a factory, a skyscraper or on a drill ground. But, somehow or other, I don't believe you'll be a policeman so very long."

Bob leaned back in his chair and drank in the invigorating air, as it whistled in through the open casement of the glass-covered porch. There was a curious twinkle in his eye, as he replied:

"I'm going to be a policeman long enough to 'get' the gangsters that 'got' me, Mr. Barton. And I believe I'm going to try a little housecleaning, or white-wings work around that neighborhood, just as a matter of sport. It doesn't hurt to try."

And Burke's jaw closed with a determined click, as he smiled grimly.

Barton was about to speak when the door from the inner ward opened behind them.

"Father! Father!" came a fresh young voice, and the old man turned around in his chair with an exclamation of delight.

"Why, Mary, my child. I'm so pleased. How did you get to see me? It's not a visiting day."

A pretty girl, whose delicate, oval face was half wreathed with waves of brown curls, leaned over the wheeled chair and kissed the old gentleman, as she placed some carnations on his lap.

She caught his hand in her own little ones and patted it affectionately.

"You dear daddy. I asked the superintendent of the hospital to let me in as a special favor to-day, for to-morrow is the regular visiting day, and I can't come then—neither can Lorna."

"Why, my dear, where are you going?"

The girl hesitated, as she noticed Burke in the wheel-chair so close at hand. By superhuman effort Bobbie was directing his attention to the distant roofs, counting the chimneys as he endeavored to keep his mind off a conversation which did not concern him.

"Oh, my dear, excuse me. Mr. Burke, turn around. I'd like to have you meet my daughter, Mary."

Bobbie willingly took the little hand, feeling a strange embarrassment as he looked up into a pair of melting blue eyes.

"It's a great pleasure," he began, and then could think of nothing more to say. Mary hesitated as well, and her father asked eagerly: "Why can't you girls come here to-morrow, my dear? By another visiting day I hope to be back home."

"Father, we have——" she hesitated, and Bobbie understood.

"I'd better be wheeling inside, Mr. Barton, and let you have the visit out here, where it's so nice. It's only my first trip, you know—so let me call my steersman."

"No secrets, no secrets," began Barton, but Bobbie had beckoned to the ward attendant. The man came out, and, at Burke's request, started to wheel him inside.

"Won't you come and visit me, sir, in my little room? I get lonely, you know, and have a lot of space. I'm so glad to have seen you, Miss Barton."

"Mr. Burke is going to be one of my very good friends, Mary. He's coming around to see us when I get back home. Won't that be pleasant?"

Mary looked at Bobbie's honest, mobile face, and saw the splendid manliness which radiated from his earnest, friendly eyes. Perhaps she saw just a trifle more in those eyes; whatever it was, it was not displeasing.

She dropped her own gaze, and softly said:

"Yes, father. He will be very welcome, if he is your friend."

On her bosom was a red rose which the florist had given her when she purchased the flowers for her father. Sometimes even florists are human, you know.

"Good afternoon; I'll see you later," said Bobbie, cheerily.

"You haven't any flowers, Mr. Burke. May I give you this little one?" asked Mary, as she unpinned the rose.

Burke flushed. He smiled, bashfully, and old Barton beamed.

"Thank you," said Bobbie, and the attendant wheeled him on into his own room.

"Nurse, could you get me a glass of water for this rose?" asked Bobbie.

"Certainly," said the pretty nurse, with a curious glance at the red blossom. "It's very pretty. It's just a bud and, if you keep it fresh, will last a long time."

She placed it on the table by his cot.

As she left the room, she looked again at the rose.

Sometimes even nurses are human.

And Bobbie looked at the rose. It was the sweetest rose he had ever seen. He hoped that it would last a long, long time.

"I will try to keep it fresh," he murmured, as he awkwardly rolled over into his bed.

Sometimes even policemen are human, too.

CHAPTER III

THE TRAIL OF THE SERPENT

Officer Burke was back again at his work on the force. He was a trifle pale, and the hours on patrol duty and fixed post seemed trebly long, for even his sturdy physique was tardy in recuperating from that vicious shock at the base of his brain.

"Take it easy, Burke," advised Captain Sawyer, "you have never had a harder day in uniform than this one. Those two fires, the work at the lines with the reserves and your patrol in place of Dexter, who is laid up with his cold, is going it pretty strong."

"That's all right, Captain. I'm much obliged for your interest. But a little more work to-night won't hurt me. I'll hurry strength along by keeping up this hustling. People who want to stay sick generally succeed. Doctor MacFarland is looking after me, so I am not worried."

Bobbie left the house with his comrades to relieve the men on patrol.

It was late afternoon of a balmy spring day.

The weeks since he had been injured had drifted into months, and there seemed many changes in the little world of the East Side. This store had failed; that artisan had moved out, and even two or three fruit dealers whom Bobbie patronized had disappeared.

In the same place stood other stands, managed by Italians who looked like caricatures drawn by the same artist who limned their predecessors.

"It must be pretty hard for even the Italian Squad to tell all these fellows apart, Tom," said Bobbie, as they stood on the corner by one of the stalls.

"Sure, lad. All Ginnies look alike to me. Maybe that's why they carve each other up every now and then at them little shindigs of theirs. Little family rows, they are, you know. I guess they add a few marks of identification, just for the family records," replied Tom Dolan, an old man on the precinct. "However, I get along with 'em all right by keeping my eye out for trouble and never letting any of 'em get me first. They're all right, as long as you smile at 'em. But they're tricky, tricky. And when you hurt a Wop's vanity it's time to get a half-nelson on your night-stick!"

They separated, Dolan starting down the garbage-strewn side street to chase a few noisy push-cart merchants who, having no other customers in view, had congregated to barter over their respective wares.

"Beat it, you!" ordered Dolan. "This ain't no Chamber of Commerce. Git!"

With muttered imprecation the peddlers pushed on their carts to make place for a noisy, tuneless hurdy-gurdy. On the pavement at its side a dozen children congregated—none over ten—to dance the turkey trot and the "nigger," according to the most approved Bowery artistry of "spieling."

"Lord, no wonder they fall into the gutter when they grow up," thought Bobbie. "They're sitting in it from the time they get out of their swaddling rags."

Bobbie walked up to the nearby fruit merchant.

"How much is this apple, Tony?"

The Italian looked at him warily, and then smirked.

"Eet's nothing toa you, signor. I'ma da policeman's friend. You taka him."

Bobbie laughed, as he fished out a nickel from his pocket. He shook his head, as he replied.

"No, Tony, I don't get my apples from the 'policeman's friend.' I can pay for them. You know all of us policemen aren't grafters—even on the line of apples and peanuts."

The Italian's eyes grew big.

"Well, you'ra de first one dat offer to maka me de pay, justa de same. Eet's a two centa, eef you insist."

He gave Bobbie his change, and the young man munched away on the fresh fruit with relish. The Italian gave him a sunny grin, and then volunteered:

"Youa de new policeman, eh?"

"I have been in the hospital for more than a month, so that's why you haven't seen me. How long have you been on this corner? There was another man here when I came this way last."

"Si, signor. That my cousin Beppo. But he's gone back to It'. He had some money—he wanta to keep eet, so he go while he can."

"What do you mean by that?"

"I don'ta wanta talk about eet, signor," said the Italian, with a strange look. "Eet'sa bad to say I was his cousin even."

The dealer looked worried, and naturally Bobbie became curious and more insistent.

"You can tell me, if it's some trouble. Maybe I can help you some time if you're afraid of any one."

The Italian shook his head, pessimistically.

"No, signor. Eet'sa better I keep what you call de mum."

"Did he blow up somebody with a bomb? Or was it stiletto work?" asked Bobbie, as he threw away the core of the apple, to observe it greedily captured by a small, dirty-faced urchin by the curb.

The fruit merchant looked into Officer Burke's face, and, as others had done, was inspired by its honesty and candor. He felt that here might be a friend in time of trouble. Most of the policemen he knew were austere and cynical. He leaned toward Burke and spoke in a subdued tone.

"Poor Beppo, he have de broken heart. He was no Black Hand—he woulda no usa de stiletto on a cheecken, he so kinda, gooda man. He justa leave disa country to keepa from de suicide."

"Why, that's strange! Tell me about it. Poor fellow!"

"He'sa engag-ed to marry de pretty Maria Cenini, de prettiest girl in our village, back in It'—excepta my wife. Beppo, he senda on de money, so she can coma dis country and marry him. Dat wasa four week ago she shoulda be here. But, signor, whena Beppo go toa de Battery to meet her froma da Ellis Island bigga boat he no finda her."

"Did she die?"

"Oh, signor, Beppo, he wisha she hadda died. He tooka de early boat to meeta her, signor, and soma ona tella de big officier at de Battery he'sa da cousin of her sweeta heart. She goa wid him, signor, and Beppo never finda her."

"Why, you don't mean the girl was abducted?"

"Signor, whatever eet was, Beppo hear from one man from our village who leeve in our village dat he see poor Maria weed her face all paint, and locked up in de tougha house in Newark two weeks ago. Oh, *madre dio*, signor, she's a da bad girl! Beppo, he nearly killa his friend for tell him, and den he go to Newark to looka for her at de house. But she gone, and poor Beppo he was de pinched for starting de fight in de house. He pay twanty-five de dols, and coma back here. De nexta morning a beeg man come to Beppo, and he say: 'Wop, you geet out dis place, eef you tella de police about dees girl,' Dassal."

Burke looked into the nervous, twitching face of the poor Italian, and realized that here was a deeper tragedy than might be guessed by a passerby. The man's eyes were wet, and he convulsively fumbled at the corduroy coat, which he had doubtless worn long before he ever sought the portals of the Land of Liberty.

"Oh, signor. Data night Beppo he was talk to de policaman, justa like me. He say no word, but dat beega man he musta watch, for desa gang-men dey busta de stand, and dey tella Beppo to geet out or dey busta heem. Beppo he tell me I can hava de stand eef I pay him some eacha week. I take it—and now I am afraid de busta me!"

Bobbie laid a comforting hand upon the man's heaving shoulder.

"There, don't you worry. Don't tell anyone else you're his cousin, and I won't either. You don't need to be afraid of these gang-men. Just be careful and yell for the police. The trouble with you Italians is that you are afraid to tell the police anything when you are treated badly. Your cousin should have reported this case to the Ellis Island authorities. They would have traced that girl and saved her."

The man looked gratefully into Burke's eyes, as the tears ran down his face.

"Oh, signor, eef all de police were lika you we be not afraid."

Just then he dropped his eyes, and Burke noticed that his hand trembled as he suddenly reached for a big orange and held it up. The man spoke with a surprising constraint, still holding his look upon the fruit.

"Signor, here's a fine orange. You wanta buy heem?" In a whisper he added: "Eet is de bigga man who told my cousin to get outa da country!"

Bobbie in astonishment turned around and beheld two pedestrians who were walking slowly past, both staring curiously at the Italian.

He gave an exclamation of surprise as he noticed that one of the men was no less a personage than Jimmie the Monk. The man with him was a big, raw-boned Bowery character of pugilistic build.

"Why, I thought that scoundrel would have been tried and sentenced by this time," murmured the officer. "I know they told me his case had been postponed by his lawyer, an alderman. But this is one on me."

The smaller man caught Burke's eye and gave him an insolent laugh. He even stopped and muttered something to his companion.

Burke's blood was up in an instant.

He advanced quickly toward the tough. Jimmie sneered, as he stood his ground, confident in the security of his political protection.

"Move on there," snapped Burke. "This is no loafing place."

"Aaaah, go chase sparrers," snarled Jimmie the Monk. "Who ye think yer talking to, rookie?"

Now, Officer Burke was a peaceful soul, despite his military training. His short record on the force had been noteworthy for his ability to disperse several incipient riots, quiet more than one brawl, and tame several bad men without resorting to rough work. But there was a rankling in his spirit which overcame the geniality which had been reigning in his heart so short a time before.

He was tired. He was weak from his recent confinement. But the fighting blood of English and some Irish ancestors stirred in his veins.

He walked quietly up to the Monk, and his voice was low, his words calm, as he remarked: "You clear out of this neighborhood. I am going to put you where you belong the first chance I get. And I don't want any of your impudence now. Move along."

Jimmie mistook the quiet manner for respect and a timid memory of the recent retirement from active service.

He spread his legs, and, with a wink to his companion, he began, with the strident rasp of tone which can seldom be heard above Fourteenth Street and east of Third Avenue.

"Say, bo. Do you recollect gittin' a little present? Well, listen, dere's a Christmas tree of dem presents comin' to you ef ye tries any more of dis stuff. I'm in *right* in dis district, don't fergit it. Ye tink's I'm going to de Island? Wipe dat off yer memory, too. W'y, say, I kin git yer buttons torn off and yer shield put in de scrap heap by de Commish if I says de woid down on Fourteenth Street, at de bailiwick."

"I know who was back of the assault on me, Monk, and let me tell you I'm going to get the man who threw it. Now, you get!"

Burke raised his right hand carelessly to the side of his collar, as he pressed up close to the gangster. The big man at his side came nearer, but as the policeman did not raise his club, which swung idly by its leather thong, to his left wrist, he was as unprepared for what happened as Jimmie.

"Why you——" began the latter, with at least six ornate oaths which out-tarred the vocabulary of any jolly, profane tar who ever swore.

Burke's hand, close to his own shoulder, and not eight inches away from Jimmie's leering jowl, closed into a very hard fist. Before the tough knew what had hit him that nearby fist had sent him reeling into the gutter from a short shoulder jab, which had behind it every ounce of weight in the policeman's swinging body.

Jimmie lay there.

The other man's hand shot to his hip pocket, but the officer's own revolver was out before he could raise the hand again. Army practice came handy to Burke in this juncture.

"Keep your hand where it is," exclaimed the policeman, "or you'll get a bullet through it."

"You dog, I'll get you sent up for this," muttered the big man.

But with his revolver covering the fellow, Burke quickly "frisked" the hip pocket and discovered the bulk of a weapon. This was enough.

"I fixed the Monk. Now, you're going up for the Sullivan Law against carrying firearms. You're number one, with me, in settling up this score!" Jimmie had shown signs of awakening from the slumber induced by Burke's sturdy right hand.

He pulled himself up as Burke marched his man around the corner. The Monk hurried, somewhat unsteadily, to the edge of the fruit stand and looked round it after the two figures.

"Do youse know dat cop, ye damn Ginnie?" muttered Jimmie.

"Signor, no!" replied the fruit dealer, nervously. "I never saw heem on dis beat before to-day, wenna he buy de apple from me."

Jimmie turned—discretion conquering temporary vengeance, and started in the opposite direction. He stopped long enough to say, as he rubbed his bruised jaw, "Well, Wop, ye ain't like to see much more of 'im around dis dump neither, an' ye ain't likely to see yerself neither, if ye do too much talkin' wid de cops."

Jimmie hurried up the street to a certain rendezvous to arrange for a rescue party of some sort. In the meantime Officer 4434 led an unwilling prisoner to the station house, one hand upon the man's right arm. His own right hand gripped his stick firmly.

"You make a wiggle and I'm going to give it to you where I got that brick, only harder," said Burke, softly.

A crowd of urchins, young men and even a few straggling women followed him with his prisoner. It grew to enormous proportions by the time he had reached the station house.

As they entered the front room Captain Sawyer looked up from his desk, where he had been checking up some reports.

"Ah, what have we this time, Burke?"

"This man is carrying a revolver in his hip pocket," declared the officer. "That will take care of him, I suppose."

Dexter, at the captain's direction, searched the man. The revolver was the first prize. In his pocket was a queer memorandum book. It contained page after page of girls' names, giving only the first name, with some curious words in cipher code after each one. In the same pocket was a long, flat parcel. Dexter handed it to the captain who opened it gingerly. Inside the officer found at least twenty-five small packets, all wrapped in white paper. He opened two of these. They contained a flaky, white powder.

The man looked down as Sawyer gave him a shrewd glance.

"We have a very interesting visitor, Burke. Thanks for bringing him in. So you're a cocaine peddler?"

The man did not reply.

"Take him out into one of the cells, Dexter. Get all the rest of his junk and wrap it up. Look through the lining of his clothes and strip him. This is a good catch, Burke."

The prisoner sullenly ambled along between two policemen, who locked him up in one of the "pens" in the rear of the front office. Burke leaned over the desk.

"He was walking with that Jimmie the Monk when I got him. Jimmie acted ugly, and when I told him to move on he began to curse me."

"What did you do?"

"I handed him an upper-cut. Then this fellow tried to get his gun. Jimmie will remember me, and I'll get him later, on something. I didn't want to call out the reserves, so I brought this man right on over here, and let Jimmie attend to himself. I suppose we'll hear from him before long."

"Yes, I see the message coming now," exclaimed Captain Sawyer in a low tone. "Don't you open your mouth. I'll do the talking now."

As he spoke, Burke followed his eyes and turned around. A large man, decorated with a shiny silk hat, shinier patent leather shoes of extreme breadth of beam, a flamboyant waistcoat, and a gold chain from which dangled a large diamond charm, swaggered into the room, mopping his red face with a silk handkerchief.

"Well, well, captain!" he ejaculated, "what's this I hear about an officer from this precinct assaulting two peaceful civilians?"

The Captain looked steadily into the puffy face of the speaker. His steely gray eyes fairly snapped with anger, although his voice was unruffled as he replied, "You'd better tell me all you heard, and who you heard it from."

The big man looked at Burke and scowled ominously. It was evident that Officer 4434 was well known to him, although Bobbie had never seen the other in his life.

"Here's the fellow. Clubbing one of my district workers—straight politics, that's what it is, or I should say crooked politics. I'm going to take this up with the Mayor this very day. You know his orders about policemen using their clubs."

"Yes, Alderman, I know that and several other things. I know that this policeman did not use his club but his fist on one of your ward heelers, and that was for cursing him in public. He should have arrested him. I also know that you are the lawyer for this gangster, Jimmie the Monk. And I know what we have on his friend. You can look at the blotter if you want. I haven't finished writing it all yet."

The Captain turned the big record-book around on his desk, while the politician angrily examined it.

"What's that? Carrying weapons, unlawfully? Carrying cocaine? Why, this is a frame-up. This man Morgan is a law-abiding citizen. You're trying to send him up to make a record for yourself. I'm going to take this up with the Mayor as sure as my name is Kelly!"

"Take it up with the United States District Attorney, too, Mr. Alderman, for I've got some other things on your man Morgan. This political stuff is beginning to wear out," snapped Sawyer. "There are too many big citizens getting interested in this dope trade and in the gang work for you and your Boss to keep it hushed any longer."

He turned to Burke and waved his hand toward the stairway which led to the dormitory above.

"Go on upstairs, my boy, and rest up a little bit. You're pale. This has been a hard day, and I'm going to send out White to relieve you. Take a little rest and then I'll send you up to Men's Night Court with Morgan, for I want him held over for investigation by the United States officers."

Alderman Kelly puffed and fumed with excitement. This was getting beyond his depths. He was a competent artist in the criminal and lower courts, but his talents for delaying the law of the Federal procedure were rather slim.

"What do you mean? I'm going to represent Morgan, and I'll have something to say about his case at Night Court. I know the magistrate."

Sawyer took out the memorandum book from the little parcel of "exhibits" removed from the prisoner.

"Well, Alderman," Burke heard him say, as he started up the stairs, "you ought to be pleased to have a long and profitable case. For I think this is just starting the trail on a round-up of some young men who have been making money by a little illegal traffic. There are about four hundred girls' names in this book, and the Chief of Detectives has a reputation for being able to figure out ciphers."

Alderman Kelly dropped his head, but gazed at Sawyer's grim face from beneath his heavy brows with a baleful intensity. Then he left the station house.

CHAPTER IV

WHAT THE DOCTOR SAID

Officer Bobbie Burke found the case at the Men's Night Court to be less difficult than his experience with Dutch Annie and her "friend." The magistrate disregarded the pleading of Alderman Kelly to show the "law-abiding" Morgan any leniency. The man was quickly bound over for investigation by the Grand Jury, upon the representations of Captain Sawyer, who went in person to look after the matter.

"This man will bear a strict investigation, Mr. Kelly, and I propose to hold him without bail until the session to-morrow. Your arguments are of no avail. We have had too much talk and too little actual results on this trafficking and cocaine business, and I will do what I can to prevent further delays."

"But, your honor, how about this brutal policeman?" began Kelly, on a new tack. "Assaulting a peaceful citizen is a serious matter, and I am prepared to bring charges."

"Bring any you want," curtly said the magistrate. "The officer was fully justified. If night-sticks instead of political pull were used on these gun-men our politics would be cleaner and our city would not be the laughing-stock of the rest of the country. Officer Burke, keep up your good work, and clean out the district if you can. We need more of it."

Burke stepped down from the stand, embarrassed but happy, for it was a satisfaction to know that there were some defenders of the police. He espied Jimmie the Monk sitting with some of his associates in the rear of the room, but this time he was prepared for trouble, as he left. Consequently, there was none.

When he returned to the station house he was too tired to return to his room in the boarding-house where he lodged, but took advantage of the proximity of a cot in the dormitory for the reserves.

Next day he was so white and fagged from the hard duty that Captain Sawyer called up Doctor MacFarland, the police surgeon for the precinct.

When the old Scotchman came over he examined. Burke carefully and shook his head sternly.

"Young man," said he, "if you want to continue on this work, remember that you have just come back from a hospital. There has been a bad shock to your nerves, and if you overdo yourself you will have some trouble with that head again. You had better ask the Captain for a little time off—take it easy this next day or two and don't pick any more fights."

"I'm not hunting for trouble, doctor. But, you know, I do get a queer feeling—maybe it is in my head, from that brick, but it feels in my heart—whenever I see one of these low scoundrels who live on the misery of their women. This Jimmie the Monk is one of the worst I have ever met, and I can't rest easy until I see him landed behind the bars."

"There is no greater curse to our modern civilization than the work of these men, Burke. It is not so much the terrible lives of the women whom they enslave; it is the disease which is scattered broadcast, and carried into the homes of working-men, to be handed to virtuous and unsuspecting wives, and by heredity to innocent children, visiting, as the Bible says, 'the iniquities of the fathers unto the third and the fourth generation.'"

The old doctor sat down dejectedly and rested his chin on his hand, as he sat talking to Burke in the rear room of the station house.

"Doctor, I've heard a great deal about the white slave traffic, as every one who keeps his ears open in the big city must. Do you think the reports are exaggerated?"

"No, my boy. I've been practicing medicine and surgery in New York for forty years. When I came over here from Scotland the city was no better than it should have been. But it was an *American* city then—not an 'international melting pot,' as the parlor sociologists proudly call it. The social evil is the oldest profession in the world; it began when one primitive man wanted that which he could not win with love, so he offered a bribe. And the bribe was taken, whether it was a carved amulet or a morsel of game, or a new fashion in furs. And the woman who took it realized that she could escape the drudgery of the other women, could obtain more bribes for her loveless barter ... and so it has grown down through the ages."

The old Scotchman lit his pipe.

"I've read hundreds of medical books, and I've had thousands of cases in real life which have taught me more than my medical books. What I've learned has not made me any happier, either. Knowledge doesn't bring you peace of mind on a subject like this. It shows you how much greed and wickedness and misery there are in the world."

"But, doctor, do you think this white slave traffic is a new development? We've only heard about it for the last two or three years, haven't we?"

The physician nodded.

"Yes, but it's been there in one form or another. It caused the ruin of the Roman Empire; it brought the downfall of mediaeval Europe, and whenever a splendid civilization springs up the curse of sex-bondage in one form or another grows with it like a cancer."

"But medicine is learning to cure the cancer. Can't it help cure this?"

"We are getting near the cure for cancer, maybe near the cure for this cancer as well. Sex-bondage was the great curse of negro slavery in the United States; it was the thing which brought misery on the South, in the carpet-bag days, as a retribution for the sins of the fathers. We cured that and the South is bigger and better for that terrible surgical operation than it ever was before. But this latest development—organized capture of ignorant, weak, pretty girls, to be held in slavery by one man or by a band of men and a few debauched old hags, is comparatively a new thing in America. It has been caused by the swarms of ignorant emigrants, by the demand of the lowest classes of those emigrants and the Americans they influence for a satisfaction of their lust. It is made easy by the crass ignorance of the country girls, the emigrant girls, and by the drudgery and misery of the working girls in the big cities."

"I saw two cases in Night Court, Doc, which explained a whole lot to me—drunken fathers and brutal husbands who poisoned their own wives—it taught that not all the blame rests upon the weakness of the women."

"Of course it doesn't," exclaimed MacFarland impetuously. "It rests upon Nature, and the way our boasted Society is mistreating Nature. Woman is weaker than man when it comes to brute force; you know it is force which does rule the world when you do get down to it, in government, in property, in business, in education—it is all survival of the strongest, not always of the fittest. A woman should be in the home; she can raise babies, for which Nature intended her. She can rule the world through her children, but when she gets out to fight hand to hand with man in the work-world she is outclassed. She can't stand the physical strain thirty days in the month; she can't stand the starvation, the mistreatment, the battling that a man gets in the world. She needs tenderness and care, for you know every normal woman is a mother-to-be—and that is the most wonderful thing in the world, the most beautiful. When the woman comes up against the stone wall of competition with men her weakness asserts itself. That's why good women fall. It's not the 'easiest way'—it's just forced upon them. As for the naturally bad women—well, that has come from some trait of another generation, some weakness which has been increased instead of cured by all this twisted, tangled thing we call modern civilization."

The doctor sighed.

"There are a lot of women in the world right now, Burke, who are fighting for what they call the 'Feminist Movement'. They don't want homes; they want men's jobs. They don't want to raise their babies in the old-fashioned way; they want the State to raise them with trained nurses and breakfast food. They don't see anything beautiful in home life, and cooking, and loving their husbands. They want the lecture platform (and the gate-receipts); they want to run the government, they want men to be breeders, like the drones in the beehive, and they don't want to be tied to one man for life. They want to visit around. The worst of it is that they are clever, they write well, they talk well, and they interest the women who are really normal, who only half-read, only half-analyze, and only get a part of the idea! These normal women are devoting, as they should, most of their energies to the normal things of woman life—children, home, charity, and neighborliness. But the clever feminist revolutionists are giving them just enough argument to make them dissatisfied. They flatter the domestic woman by telling her she is not enough appreciated, and that she should control the country. They lead the younger women away from the old ideals of love and home and religion; in their place they would substitute selfishness, loose morals, and will change the chivalry, which it has taken men a thousand years to cultivate, into brutal methods, when men realize that women want absolute equality. Then, should such a condition ever be accepted by society in general, we will do away with the present kind of social evil—to have a tidal wave of lust."

Bobbie listened with interest. It was evident that Doctor MacFarland was opening up a subject close to his heart. The old man's eyes sparkled as he continued.

"You asked about the traffic in women, as we hear of it in New York. Well, the only way we can cure it is to educate the men of all classes so that for reasons moral, sanitary, and feelings of honest pride in themselves they will not patronize the market where souls are sought. This can't be done by passing laws, but by better books, better ways of amusement, better living conditions for working people, so that they will not be 'driven to drink' and what follows it to forget their troubles. Better factories and kinder treatment to the great number of workmen, with fairer wage scale would bring nearer the possibility of marriage—which takes not one, but two people out of the danger of the gutter. Minimum wage scales and protection of working women would make the condition of their lives better, so that they would not be forced into the streets and brothels to make their livings.

"Why, Burke, a magistrate who sits in Night Court has told me that medical investigation of the street-walkers he has sentenced revealed the fact that nine of every ten were diseased. When the men who foolishly think they are good 'sports' by debauching with these women learn that they are throwing away the health of their wives and children to come, as well as risking the contagion of diseases which can only be bottled up by medical treatment but never completely cured; when it gets down to the question of men buying and selling these poor women as they undoubtedly do, the only way to check that is for every decent man in the country to help in the fight. It is a man evil; men must slay it. Every procurer in the country should be sent to prison, and every house of ill fame should be closed."

"Don't you think the traffic would go on just the same, doctor? I have heard it said that in European cities the authorities confined such women to certain parts of the city. Then they are subjected to medical examination as well."

"No, Burke, segregation will not cure it. Many of the cities abroad have given that up. The medical examinations are no true test, for they are only partially carried out—not all the women will admit their sinful ways of life, nor submit to control by the government. The system prevails in Paris and in Germany, and there is more disease there than in any other part of Europe. Men, depending upon the imaginary security of a doctor's examination card, abandon themselves the more readily, and caution is thrown to the winds, with the result that a woman who has been O.K.'d by a government physician one day may contract a disease and spread it the very next day. You can depend upon it that if she has done so she will evade the examination next time in order not to interfere with her trade profits. So, there you are. This is an ugly theme, but we must treat it scientifically.

"You know it used to be considered vulgar to talk about the stomach and other organs which God gave us for the maintenance of life. But when folks began to realize that two-thirds of the sickness in the world, contagious and otherwise, resulted from trouble with the stomach, that false modesty had to give way. Consequently to-day we have fewer epidemics, much better general health, because men and women understand how to cure many of their own ailments with prompt action and simple methods.

"The vice problem is one which reaps its richest harvest when it is protected from the sunlight. Sewers are not pleasant table-talk, but they must be watched and attended by scientific sanitary engineers. A cancer of the intestines is disagreeable to think about. But when it threatens a patient's life the patient should know the truth and the doctor should operate. Modern society is the patient, and death-dealing sex crimes are the cancerous growth, which must be operated upon. Whenever we allow a neighborhood to maintain houses of prostitution, thus regulating and in a way sanctioning the evil, we are granting a sort of corporation charter for an industry which is run upon business methods. And business, you know, is based upon filling the 'demand,' with the necessary 'supply.' And the manufacturers, in this case, are the procurers and the proprietresses of these houses. There comes in the business of recruiting—and hence the traffic in souls, as it has aptly been called. No, my boy, government regulation will never serve man, nor woman, for it cannot cover all the ground. As long as women are reckless, lazy and greedy, yielding to temporary, half-pleasant sin rather than live by work, you will find men with low ideals in all ranks of life who prefer such illicit 'fun' to the sweetness of wedlock! Why, Burke, sex is the most beautiful thing in the world—it puts the blossoms on the trees, it colors the butterflies' wings, it sweetens the songs of the birds, and it should make life worth living for the worker in the trench, the factory hand, the office toiler and the millionaire. But it will never do so until people understand it, know how to guard it with decent knowledge, and sanctify it morally and hygienically."

The old doctor rose and knocked the ashes out of his briar pipe. He looked at the eager face of the young officer.

"But there, I'm getting old, for I yield to the melody of my own voice too much. I've got office hours, you know, and I'd better get back to my pillboxes. Just excuse an old man who is too talkative sometimes, but remember that what I've said to you is not my own old-fashioned notion, but a little boiled-down philosophy from the writings of the greatest modern scientists."

"Good-bye, Doctor MacFarland. I'll not forget it. It has answered a lot of questions in my mind."

Bobbie went to the front door of the station house with the old gentleman, and saluted as a farewell.

"What's he been chinning to you about, Burke?" queried the Captain. "Some of his ideas of reforming the world? He's a great old character, is Doc."

"I think he knows a lot more about religion than a good many ministers I've heard," replied Bobbie. "He ought to talk to a few of them."

"Sure. But they wouldn't listen if he did. They're too busy getting money to send to the heathens in China, and the niggers in Africa to bother about the heathens and poor devils here. I'm pretty strong for Doc MacFarland, even though I don't get all he's talking about."

"Say, Burke, the Doc got after me one day and gave me a string of books as long as your arm to read," put in Dexter. "He seems to think a cop ought to have as much time to read as a college boy!"

"You let me have the list, Dexter, and I'll coach you up on it," laughed Burke.

"To-day is your relief, Burke," said the Captain. "You can go up to the library and wallow in literature if you want to."

Burke smiled, as he retorted:

"I'm going to a better place to do my reading—and not out of books either, Cap."

He changed his clothes, and soon emerged in civilian garb. He had never paid his call on John Barton, although he had been out of the hospital for several days. The old man's frequent visits to him in his private room at the hospital, after that first memorable meeting, had ripened their friendship. Barton had told him of a number of new ideas in electrical appliances, and Burke was anxious to see what progress had been made since the old fellow returned to his home.

Officer 4434 was also anxious to see another member of his family, and so it was with a curious little thrill of excitement, well concealed, however, with which he entered the modest apartment of the Bartons' that evening.

"Well, well, well!" exclaimed the old man, as the young officer took his hand. "We thought you had forgotten us completely. Mary has asked me several times if you had been up to see me. I suppose you have been busy with those gangsters, and keep pretty close since you returned to active service."

Bobbie nodded.

"Yes, sir. They are always with us, you know. And a policeman does not have very much time to himself, particularly if he lolls around in bed with a throb in the back of the head, during his off hours, as I've been foolish enough to do."

"Oh, how are you feeling, Mr. Burke?" exclaimed Mary, as she entered from the rear room.

She held out her hand, and Bobbie trembled a trifle as he took her soft, warm fingers in his own.

"I'm improving, and don't believe I was ever laid up—it was just imagination on my part," answered Burke. "But I have a faded rose to make me remember that some of it was a pleasant imagination, at any rate."

Mary laughed softly, and dropped her eyes ever so slightly. But the action betrayed that she had not forgotten either.

Old Barton busied himself with some papers on a table by the side of his wheel-chair, for he was a diplomat.

"Well, now, Mr. Burke—what are your adventures? I read every day of some policeman jumping off a dock in the East River to rescue a suicide, or dragging twenty people out of a burning tenement, and am afraid that it's you. It's all right to be a hero, you know, but there's a great deal of truth in that old saying about it being better to have people remark, 'There he goes,' than 'Doesn't he look natural.'"

Bobbie took the comfortable armchair which Mary drew up.

"I haven't had anything really worth while telling about," said Burke. "I see a lot of sad things, and it makes a man feel as though he were a poor thing not to be able to improve conditions."

"That's true of every walk in life. But most people don't look at the sad any longer than they can help. I've not been having a very jolly time of it myself, but I hope for a lot of good news before long. Why don't you bring Lorna in to meet Mr. Burke, Mary?"

The girl excused herself, and retired.

"How are your patents?" asked Bobbie, with interest. "I hope you can show tricks to the Gresham people."

The old man sighed. He took up some drawings and opened a little drawer in the table.

"No, Mr. Burke, I am afraid my tricks will be slow. I have received no letter from young Gresham in reply to one I wrote him, asking to be given a salary for mechanical work here in my home. Every bit of my savings has been exhausted. You know I educated my daughters to the limit of my earnings, since my dear wife died. They have hard sledding in front of them for a while, I fear."

He hesitated, and then continued:

"Do you remember the day you met Mary? She started to say that she and Lorna could not see me on visiting day. Well, the dear girls had secured a position as clerks in Monnarde's big candy store up on Fifth Avenue. They talked it over between them, and decided that it was better for them to get to work, to relieve my mind of worry. It's the first time they ever worked, and they are sticking to it gamely. But it makes me feel terribly. Their mother never had to work, and I feel as though I have been a failure in life—to have done as much as I have, and yet not have enough in my old age to protect them from the world."

"There, there, Mr. Barton. I don't agree with you. There is no disgrace in womanly work; it proves what a girl is worth. She learns the value of money, which before that had merely come to her without a question from her parents. And you have been a splendid father ... that's easily seen from the fine sort of girl Miss Mary is."

Mary had stepped into the room with her younger sister as he spoke. They hesitated at the kindly words, and Mary drew her sister back again, her face suffused with a rosiness which was far from unhappy in its meaning.

"Well, I am very proud of Mary and Lorna. If this particular scheme works out they will be able to buy their candy at Monnarde's instead of selling it."

Bobbie rose and leaned over the table.

"What is it? I'm not very good at getting mechanical drawings. It looks as though it ought to be very important from all the wheels," he said, with a smile of interest.

Spreading out the largest of his drawings, old Barton pointed out the different lines.

"This may look like a mince pie of cogs here, but when it is put into shape it will be a simple little arrangement. This is a recording instrument which combines the phonograph and the dictagraph. One purpose—the most practical, is that a business man may dictate his letters and memoranda while sitting at his desk, in his office, instead of having a machine with a phonograph in his private office taking up space and requiring the changing of records by the dictator—which is necessary with the present business phonograph. All that will be necessary is for him to speak into a little disc. The sound waves are carried by a simple arrangement of wiring into his outer office, or wherever his stenographer works. There, where the space is presumably cheaper and easier of access than the private office, the receiving end of the machine is located. Instead of one disc at a time—limited to a certain number of letters—the machine has a magazine of discs, something like the idea of a repeating letter. Automatically the disc, which is filled, is moved up and a fresh disc takes its place. This goes on indefinitely, as you might say. A man can dictate two hundred letters, speaking as rapidly as he thinks. He never has to bother over changing his records. The girl at the other end of the wire does that when the machine registers that the supply is being exhausted. She in turn uses the discs on the regular business phonograph, or, as this is intended for large offices, where there are a great many letters, and consequently a number of stenographers, she can assign the records to the different typists."

"Why, that is wonderful, Mr. Barton!" exclaimed Burke. "It ought to make a fortune for you if it is backed and financed right. Why didn't anyone think of it before?"

Barton smiled, and caressed his drawing affectionately.

"Mr. Burke, the Patent Office is maintained for men who think up things that some fellow should have thought of before! The greatest inventions are apparently the simplest. That's what makes them hard to invent!"

He pointed to another drawing.

"That has a business value, too, and I hope to get the proper support when I have completed my models. You know, a scientific man can see all these things on the paper, but to the man with money they are pipe dreams until he sees the wheels go 'round."

He now held out his second drawing, which was easier to understand, for it was a sketch of his appliance, showing the outer appearance, and giving a diagonal section of a desk or room, with a wire running through a wall into another compartment.

"Here is where the scientist yields to his temperament and wastes a lot of time on something which probably will never bring him a cent. This is a combination of my record machine, which will be of interest to your profession."

Bobbie examined it closely, but could not divine its purpose.

"It is the application of the phonographic record to the dictagraph, so that police and detective work can be absolutely recorded, without the shadow of a doubt remaining in the minds of a trial jury or judge. Maybe this is boring you?"

"No, no—go on!"

"Well, when dictagraphs are used for the discovery of criminals it has been necessary to keep expert stenographers, and at least one other witness at the end of the wire to put down the record. Frequently the stenographer cannot take the words spoken as fast as he should to make the record. Sometimes it is impossible to get the stenographer and the witness on the wire at the exact time. Of course, this is only a crazy idea. But it seems to me that by a little additional appliance which I have planned, the record machine could be put into a room nearby, or even another house. If a certain place were under suspicion the machine could rest with more ease, less food and on smaller wages than a detective and stenographer on salary. When any one started to talk in this suspected room the vibrations of the voices would start a certain connection going through this additional wire, which would set the phonograph into action. As long as the conversation continued the records would be running continuously. No matter how rapidly words are uttered the phonograph would get them, and could be run, for further investigation, as slowly and as many times as desired. When the conversation stopped the machine would automatically blow its own dinner whistle and adjourn the meeting until the talk began again. This would take the record of at least an hour's conversation: another attachment would send in a still-alarm to the detective agency or police station, so that within that hour a man could be on the job with a new supply of records and bait the trap again."

"Wonderful!"

"Yes, and the most important part is that this is the only way of keeping a record which cannot be called a 'frame-up'—for it is a photograph of the sound waves. A grafter, a murderer, or any other criminal could be made to speak the same words in court as were put on the phonographic record, and his voice identified beyond the shadow of a doubt!"

Bobbie clapped his hand on the old man's shoulder.

"Why, Mr. Barton, that is the greatest invention ever made for capturing and convicting criminals. It's wonderful! The Police Departments of the big cities should buy enough machines to make you rich, for you could demand your own price."

Barton looked dreamily toward the window, through which twinkled the distant lights of the city streets.

"I want money, Burke, as every sane man does. But this pet of mine means more than money. I want to contribute my share to justice just as you do yours. Who knows, some day it may reward me in a way which no money could ever repay. You never can tell about such things. Who knows?"

CHAPTER V

ROSES AND THORNS

Mary's sister was as winsome and fair as she, but to Burke's keen eyes she was a weaker girl. There was a suggestion of too much attention to dress, a self-consciousness tinged with self-appreciation.

When she was introduced to Bobbie he could feel instinctively an undercurrent of condescension, ever so slight, yet perceptible to the sensitive young fellow.

"You're the first policeman I've ever met," began Lorna, with a smile, "and I really don't half believe you are one. I always think of them as swinging clubs and taking a handful of peanuts off a stand, as they walk past a corner cart. Really, I do."

Burke reddened, but retorted, amiably enough.

"I don't like peanuts, for they always remind me of the Zoo, and I never liked Zoos! But I plead guilty to swinging a club when occasion demands. You know even millionaires have their clubs, and so you can't deny us the privilege, can you?"

Lorna laughed, and gracefully pushed back a stray curl with her pretty hand. Mary frowned a bit, but trusted that Bobbie had not noticed the lack of tact.

"I've seen policemen tugging at a horse's head and getting nearly trampled to death to save some children in a runaway carriage. That was on Fifth Avenue yesterday, just when we quit work, Lorna." She emphasized the word "work," and Bobbie liked her the more for it. "And, last winter, I saw two of them taking people out on a fire-escape, wet, and covered with icicles, in a big fire over there on Manhattan Avenue. They didn't look a bit romantic, Lorna, and they even had red faces and pug noses. But I think that's a pleasanter memory than shoplifting from peanut stands."

Lorna smiled winningly, however, and sat down, not without a decorative adjustment of her pretty silk dress. Bobbie forgave her, principally because she looked so much like Mary.

They chatted as young people will, while old Barton mumbled and studied over his drawings, occasionally adding a detail, and calculating on a pad as though he were working out some problem in algebra.

Lorna's chief topic was the theater and dancing.

Mary endeavored to bring the conversation around to other things.

"I have to admit that I'm very green on theaters, Miss Barton," said Bobbie to the younger sister. "I love serious plays, and these old-fashioned kind of comedies, which teach a fellow that there's some happiness in life——but, I don't get the time to attend them. My station is down on the East Side, and I see so much tragedy and unhappiness that it has given me about all the real-life plays I could want, since I came to the police work."

Lorna scoffed, and tossed her curls.

"Oh, I don't like that stupid old stuff myself. I like the musical comedies that have dancing, and French dresses, and cleverness. I think all the serious plays nowadays are nothing but scandal—a girl can't go to see them without blushing and wishing she were at home."

"I don't agree with you, Lorna. There are some things in life that a girl should learn. An unpleasant play is likely to leave a bad taste in one's mouth, but that bad taste may save her from thinking that evil can be honey-coated and harmless. Why, the show we saw the other night—those costumes, those dances, and the songs! There was nothing left to imagine. They stop serious plays, and ministers preach sermons about them, while the musical comedies that some of the managers produce are a thousand times worse, for they teach only a bad lesson."

As Lorna started to reply the bell rang and Mary went to the door.

Two young men were outside and, at Mary's stiff invitation, they entered. Burke rose, politely.

"Why, how do you do, Mr. Baxter?" exclaimed Lorna, enthusiastically, as she extended one hand and arranged that disobedient lock of hair with the other. "Come right in, this is such a pleasant surprise."

Baxter advanced, and introduced his companion.

"This is my friend, Reggie Craig, Miss Barton. We're just on our way down to Dawley's for a little supper and a dance afterward. You know they have some great tangoing there, and I know you like it."

Lorna introduced Craig and Baxter to the others. As she came to Bobbie she said, "This is Mr. Burke. You wouldn't believe it, but he is a——"

"Friend of father's," interrupted Mary, with a look which did not escape either Bobbie or Lorna. "Won't you sit down, gentlemen?"

Burke was studying the two men with his usual rapidity of observation.

Baxter was tall, with dark, curly hair, carefully plastered straight back from a low, narrow forehead. His grooming was immaculate: his "extreme" cutaway coat showed a good physique, but the pallor of the face above it bespoke dissipation of the strength of that natural endowment. His shoes, embellished with pearl buttons set with rhinestones, were of the latest vogue, described in the man-who-saw column of the theater programmes. He looked, for all the world, like an advertisement for ready-tailored suitings.

His companion was slighter in build but equally fastidious in appearance. When he drew a handkerchief from his cuff Bobbie completed the survey and walked over toward old Barton, to look at the more interesting drawings.

"You girls must come along to Dawley's, you simply must, you know," began Baxter, still standing. "Of course, we'd be glad to have your father's friend, if he likes dancing."

"That's very kind of you, but you know I've a lot to talk about with Mr. Barton," answered Bobbie, quietly.

"May we go, father?" asked Lorna, impetuously.

"Well, I thought," said the old gentleman, "I thought that you'd——"

"Father, I haven't been to a dance or a supper since you were injured. You know that," pouted Lorna.

"What do you want to do, Mary dear?" asked the old man, helplessly.

"It's very kind of Mr. Baxter, but you know we have a guest."

Mary quietly sat down, while Lorna's temper flared.

"Well, I'm going anyway. I'm tired of working and worrying. I want to have pleasure and music and entertainment like thousands of other girls in New York. I owe it to myself. I don't intend to sit around here and talk about tenement fires and silly old patents."

Burke was embarrassed, but not so the visiting fashion plates. Baxter and Craig merely smiled at each other with studied nonchalance; they seemed used to such scenes, thought Bobbie.

Lorna flounced angrily from the room, while her father wiped his forehead with a trembling hand.

"Why, Lorna," he expostulated weakly. But Lorna reappeared with a pretty evening wrap and her hat in her hand. She donned the hat, twisting it to a coquettish angle, and Baxter unctuously assisted her to place the wrap about her shoulders.

"Lorna, I forbid your going out at this time of the evening with two gentlemen we have never met before," cried Mary.

But Lorna opened the door and wilfully left the room, followed by Craig. Baxter turned as he left, and smiled sarcastically.

"Good-*night*!" he remarked, with a significant accent on the last word.

Mary's face was white, as she looked appealingly at Burke. He tried to comfort her in his quiet way.

"I wouldn't worry, Miss Mary. I think they are nice young fellows, and you know young girls are the same the world over. I am sure they are all right, and will look after her—you know, some people do think a whole lot of dancing and jolly company, and it is punishment for them to have to talk all the time on serious things. I don't blame her, for I'm poor company—and only a policeman, after all."

John Barton looked disconsolately at the door which had slammed after the trio.

"You do think it's all right, don't you, Burke?"

"Why, certainly," said Burke. He lied like a gentleman and a soldier.

Old Barton was ill at ease, although he endeavored to cover his anxiety with his usual optimism.

"We are too hard on the youngsters, I fear," he began. "It's true that Lorna has not had very much pleasure since I was injured. The poor child has had many sleepless nights of worry since then, as well. You know she has always been our baby, while my Mary here has been the little mother since my dear wife left us."

Mary forced a smiling reply: "You dear daddy, don't worry. I know Lorna's fine qualities, and I wish we could entertain more for her than we do right in our little flat. That's one of the causes of New York's unnatural life. In the small towns and suburbs girls have porches and big parlors, while they live in a surrounding of trees and flowers. They have home music, jolly gatherings about their own pianos; we can't afford even to rent a piano just now. So, there, daddy, be patient and forgive Lorna's thoughtlessness."

Barton's face beamed again, as he caressed his daughter's soft brown curls, when she leaned over his chair to kiss him.

"My blessed little Mary: you are as old as your mother—as old as all motherhood, in your wisdom. I feel more foolishly a boy each day, as I realize the depth of your devotion and love."

Burke's eyes filled with tears, which he manfully wiped away with a sneaking little movement of his left hand, as he pretended to look out of the window toward the distant lights. A man whose tear-ducts have dried with adolescence is cursed with a shriveled soul for the rest of his life.

"Now, we mustn't let our little worry make you feel badly, Mr. Burke. Do you know, I've been thinking about a little matter in which you are concerned? Why don't you have your interests looked after in your home town?"

"My uncle? Well, I am afraid that's a lost cause. I went to the family lawyer when I returned from my army service, and he charged me five dollars for advising me to let the matter go. He said that law was law, and that the whole matter had been ended, that I had no recourse. I think I'll just stick to my work, and let my uncle get what pleasure he can out of his treatment of me."

"That is a great mistake. If he was your family lawyer, it is very possible that your uncle anticipated your going to him. And some lawyers have elastic notions of what is possible—depending upon the size of your fee. Now, I have a young friend down town. He is a patent lawyer, and I trust him. Why don't you let him look into this matter. I have given him other cases before, through my connections with the Greshams. He proved honorable and energetic. Let me write you out a letter of introduction."

"Perhaps you are right. I appreciate your advice and it will do no harm to let him try his best," said Bobbie. "I'll give him the facts and let him investigate matters."

The old man wrote a note while Burke and Mary became better acquainted. Even in her attempt to speak gaily and happily, Bobbie could discern her worriment. As Barton finished his writing, handing the envelope to Burke, the younger man decided to take a little initiative of his own.

"It's late, Mr. Barton. I have had a pleasant evening, and I hope I may have many more. But you know I promised Doctor MacFarland, the police surgeon, that I would go to bed early on the days when I was off duty. So I had better be getting back down town."

They protested cordially, but Bobbie was soon out on the street, walking toward the Subway.

He did not take the train for his own neighborhood, however. Instead he boarded a local which stopped at Sixty-sixth Street, the heart of what is called the "New Tenderloin."

In this district are dozens of dance halls, flashy restaurants and *cafés chantantes*. A block from the Subway exit was the well-known establishment called "Dawley's." This was the destination of Baxter and Craig, with Lorna Barton. Bobbie thought it well to take an observation of the social activities of these two young men.

He entered the big, glittering room, his coat and hat rudely jerked from his arms by a Greek check boy, at the doorway, without the useless formula of request.

The tables were arranged about the walls, leaving an open space in the center for dancing. Nearly every chair was filled, while the popping of corks and the clinking of glasses even so early in the evening testified to the popularity of Dawley's.

"They seem to prefer this sort of thing to theaters," thought Bobbie. "Anyway, this crowd is funnier than most comedies I've seen."

He looked around him, after being led to a corner seat by the obsequious head waiter. There was a preponderance of fat old men and vacuous looking young girls of the type designated on Broadway as "chickens." Here and there a slumming party was to be seen—elderly women and ill-at-ease men, staring curiously at the diners and dancers; young married couples who seemed to be enjoying their self-thrilled deviltry and new-found freedom. An orchestra of negro musicians were rattling away on banjos, mandolins, and singing obligatos in deep-voiced improvisations. The drummer and the cymbalist were the busiest of all; their rattling, clanging, banging addition to the music gave it an irresistible rhythmic cadence. Even Burke felt the call of the dance, until he studied the evolutions of the merrymakers. Oddly assorted couples, some in elaborate evening dress, women in shoulderless, sleeveless, backless gowns, men in dinner-coats, girls in street clothes with yard-long feathers, youths in check suits, old men in staid business frock coats—what a motley throng! All were busily engaged in the orgy of a bacchanalian dance in which couples reeled and writhed, cheek to cheek, feet intertwining, arms about shoulders. Instead of enjoying themselves the men seemed largely engaged in counting their steps, and watching their own feet whenever possible: the girls kept their eyes, for the most part, upon the mirrors which covered the walls, each watching her poises and swings, her hat, her curls, her lips, with obvious complacency.

Burke was nauseated, for instead of the old-time fun of a jolly dance, this seemed some weird, unnatural, bestial, ritualistic evolution.

"And they call this dancing?" he muttered. "But, I wonder where Miss Lorna is?"

He finally espied her, dancing with Baxter. The latter was swinging his arms and body in a snakey, serpentine one-step, as he glided down the floor, pushing other couples out of the way. Lorna, like the other girls, lost no opportunity to admire her own reflection in the mirrors.

Burke was tempted to rush forward and intercede, to pull her out of the arms of the repulsive Baxter. But he knew how foolish he would appear, and what would be the result of such an action.

As he looked the waiter approached for his order.

Burke took the menu, decorated with dancing figures which would have seemed more appropriate for some masquerade ball poster, for the Latin Quarter, and began to read the *entrees*.

As he looked down two men brushed past his table, and a sidelong glance gave him view of a face which made him quickly forget the choice of food.

It was Jimmie the Monk, flashily dressed, debonnaire as one to the manor born, talking with Craig, the companion of Baxter.

Burke held the menu card before his face. He was curious to hear the topic of their conversation. When he did so—the words were clear and distinct, as Baxter and Jimmie sat down at a table behind him—his heart bounded with horror.

"Who's dis new skirt, Craig?"

"Oh, it's a kid Baxter picked up in Monnarde's candy store. It's the best one he's landed yet, but we nearly got in Dutch to-night when we went up to her flat to bring her out. Her old man and her sister were there with some nut, and they didn't want her to go. But Baxter "lamped" her, and she fell for his eyes and sneaked out anyway. You better keep off, Jimmie, for you don't look like a college boy—and that's the gag Baxter's been giving her. She thinks she's going to a dance at the Yale Club next week. It's harder game than the last one, but we'll get it fixed to-night. You better send word to Izzie to bring up his taxi—in about an hour."

"I'll go now, Craig. Tell Baxter dat it'll be fixed. Where'll he take her?"

Craig replied in a low tone, which thwarted Burke's attempt to eavesdrop.

CHAPTER VI

THE WORK OF THE GANGSTERS

Bobbie Burke's eyes sparkled with the flame of battle spirit, yet he maintained an outward calm. He turned his face toward the wall of the restaurant while Jimmie the Monk tripped nonchalantly out into the street. Burke did not wish to be recognized too soon. The negro musicians struck up a livelier tune than before. The dancing couples bobbed and writhed in the sensuous, shameless intimacies of the demi-mondaine bacchante. The waiters merrily juggled trays, stacked skillfully with vari-colored drinks, and bumped the knees of the close-sitting guests with silvered champagne buckets. Popping corks resounded like the distant musketry of the crack sharp-shooters of the Devil's Own. Indeed, this was an ambuscade of the greatest, oldest, cruellest, most blood-thirsty conflict of civilized history—the War of the Roses—the Massacre of the Innocents! In Bobbie's ears the jangling tambourine, the weird splutterings of the banjos, the twanging of the guitars, the shrill music of the violins and clarionet, the monotonous rag-time pom-pom of the piano accompanist, the clash and bang of cymbal and base-drum, the coarse minor cadences of the negro singers—all so essential to cabaret dancing of this class—sounded like the war pibroch of a Satanic clan of reincarnate fiends.

The waiter was serving some savory viands, for such establishments cater cleverly to the beast of the dining room as well as of the boudoir.

But Burke was in no mood to eat or drink. His soul was sickened, but his mind was working with lightning acumen.

"Bring me my check now as I may have to leave before you come around again," he directed his waiter.

"Yes, sir, certainly," responded the Tenderloin Dionysius, not without a shade of regret in his cackling voice. Early eaters and short stayers reduced the percentage on tips, while moderate orders of drinks meant immoderate thrift—to the waiter.

The check was forthcoming at once. Burke quietly corrected the addition of the items to the apparent astonishment of the waiter. He produced the exact change, while a thunder-storm seemed imminent on the face of his servitor. Burke, however, drew forth a dollar bill from his pocket, and placed it with the other change, smiling significantly.

"Oh, sir, thank you"—began the waiter, surprised into the strictly unprofessional weakness of an appreciation.

Bobbie, with a left-ward twitch of his head, and a slight quiver of the lid of his left eye, brought an attentive ear close to his mouth.

"My boy, I want you to go outside and have the taxicab starter reserve a machine for 'Mr. Green.' Tell him to have it run forward and clear of the awning in front of the restaurant—slip him this other dollar, now, and impress on him that I want that car about twenty-five feet to the right of the door as you go out."

The waiter nodded, and leered slyly.

"All right, sir—I get ye, Mr. Green. It's a quick getaway, is that it?"

"Exactly," answered Bobbie, "and I want the chauffeur to have all his juice on—the engine cranked and ready for another Vanderbilt Cup Race." Bobbie gave the waiter one of his best smiles—behind that smile was a manful look, a kindliness of character and a great power of purpose, which rang true, even to this blasé and cynical dispenser of the grape. The latter nodded and smiled, albeit flabbily, into the winsome eyes of the young officer.

"Ye're a reg'lar fellar, Mr. Green, I kin see that! Trust me to have a lightning conductor fer you—with his lamps lit and burning. These nighthawk taxis around here make most of their mazuma by this fly stuff—generally the souses ain't got enough left for a taxicab, and it's a waste o' time stickin' 'em up since the rubes are so easy with the taxi meter. But just look out for a little badger work on the chauffeur when ye git through with 'im."

Burke nodded. Then he added. "Just keep this to yourself, won't you? There's nothing crooked about it—I'm trying to do some one a good turn. Tell them to keep the taxi ready, no matter how long it takes."

"Sure and I will, Mr. Green."

The waiter walked away toward the front door, where he carried out Burke's instructions, slipping the second bill into the willing hand of the starter.

As he came back he shrewdly studied the face of the young policeman who was quietly listening to the furious fusillade of the ragtime musicians.

"Well, that guy's not as green as he says his name is. He don't look like no crook, neither! I wonder what his stall is? Well, *I* should worry!"

And he went his way rejoicing in the possession of that peace of mind which comes to some men who let neither the joys nor woes of others break through the armament of their own comfortable placidity. Every night of his life was crowded with curious, sad and ridiculous incidents; had he let them linger long in his mind his hand and temperament would have suffered a loss of accumulative skill. That would have spelled ruin, and this particular waiter, like so many of his flabby-faced brothers, was a shrewd tradesman—in the commodities of his discreetly elastic memory—and the even more valuable asset, a talent for forgetting!

Burke was biding his time, and watching developments.

He saw the mealy-faced Baxter take Lorna out upon the dancing floor for the next dance. They swung into the rhythm of the dance with easy familiarity, which proved that the girl was no novice in this style of terpsichorean enjoyment.

"She has been to other dances like this," muttered Bobbie as he watched with a strange loathing in his heart. "It's terrible to see the girls of a great modern city like New York entering publicly into a dance which I used to see on the Barbary Coast in 'Frisco. If they had seen it danced out there I don't believe they'd be so anxious to imitate it now."

Lorna and Baxter returned through the crowded merrymakers to their seats, and sat down at the table.

"You need another cocktail," suggested Baxter, after sipping one himself and forgetting the need for reserve in his remarks. "You mustn't be a bum sport at a dance like this, Miss Barton."

"Oh, Mr. Baxter, I don't dare go home with a breath like cocktails. You know Mary and I sleep together," objected Lorna.

"Don't worry about that, little girlie," said Baxter. "She won't mind it to-night."

To Burke's keen ears there was a shade of hidden menace in the words.

"Come on, now, just this one," said Baxter coaxingly. "It won't hurt. There's always room for one more."

What a temptation it was for the muscular policeman to swing around and shake the miserable wretch as one would a cur!

But Bobbie had learned the value of controlling his temper; that is one of the first requisites of a policeman's as well as of an army man's life.

"Do you know, Mr. Baxter," said Lorna, after she had yielded to the insistence of her companion, "that cocktail makes me a little dizzy. I guess it will take me a long while to get used to such drinks. You know, I've been brought up in an awfully old-fashioned way. My father would simply kill me if he thought I drank beer—and as for cocktails and highballs and horse's necks, and all those real drinks ... well, I hate to think of it. Ha! ha!"

And she laughed in a silly way which made Burke know that she was beginning to feel the effect.

"I wonder if I hadn't better assert myself right now?" he mused, pretending to eat a morsel. "It would cause a commotion, but it would teach her a lesson, and would teach her father to keep a closer watch."

Just then he heard his own name mentioned by the girl behind.

"Say, Mr. Baxter, you came just at the right time to-night. That Burke who was calling on father is a stupid policeman, whom he met in the hospital, and I was being treated to a regular sermon about life and wickedness and a lot of tiresome rot. I don't like policemen, do you?"

"I should say not!" was Baxter's heartfelt answer.

They were silent an instant.

"A policeman, you say, eh?"

"Yes; I certainly don't think he's fit to call on nice people. The next think we know father will have firemen and cab-drivers and street cleaners, I suppose. They're all in the same class to me—just servants."

"What precinct did he come from?"

Baxter's tone was more earnest than it had been.

Burke's face reddened at the girl's slur, but he continued his waiting game.

"Precinct? What's that? I don't know where he came from. He's a New York policeman, that's all I found out. It didn't interest me, why should it you? Oh, Mr. Baxter, look at that beautiful willow plume on that girl's hat. She is a silly-looking girl, but that is a wonderful hat."

Baxter grunted and seemed lost in thought.

Burke espied Jimmie the Monk meandering through the tables, in company with a heavy, smooth-faced man whose eyes were directed from even that distance toward the table at which Lorna sat.

Burke wiped his forehead with his handkerchief, thus cutting off Jimmie's possible view of his features.

"Ah, Jimmie, back again. And I see you're with my old friend, Sam Shepard!"

Baxter rose to shake hands with the newcomer. He introduced him to Lorna, backing close against Burke's shoulder as he did so.

"This is my friend, Sam Shepard, the theatrical manager, Miss Lorna," began Baxter. "He's the man who can get you on the stage. You know I was telling you about him. This is Miss Barton, you've heard about, Sam. Sit down and tell her about your new comic opera that you're casting now."

"THIS IS MY FRIEND, SAM SHEPARD, THE THEATRICAL MANAGER, MISS LORNA. HE'S THE MAN WHO CAN GET YOU ON THE STAGE."
p. 108

"This is my friend, Sam Shepard, the theatrical manager, Miss Lorna. He's the man who can get you on the stage.

As Shepard shook Lorna's hand, Jimmie leaned over toward Baxter's ear to whisper. They were not two feet from Burke's own ears, so he heard the message: "I've got de taxi ready. Now, make a good getaway to Reilly's house, Baxter."

"Say, Jimmie, just a minute," murmured Baxter. "This girl says a cop was up calling on her father. I met the guy. His name was Burke. Do you know him? Is he apt to queer anything?"

Jimmie the Monk started.

"Burke? What did he look like?"

"Oh, pretty slick-looking gink. Well set-up—looked like an army man, and gave me a hard stare when he lamped me. Had been in the hospital with the old fellow."

"Gee, dat's Burke, de guy dat's been after me, and I'm goin' ter do 'im. Is he buttin' in on dis?"

"Yes; what about him? You're not scared of him, are you?"

"Naw; but he's a bad egg. Say, he's a rookie dat t'inks 'e kin clean up our gang. Now, you better dish dis job and let Shepard pull de trick. Take it from yer Uncle Jim!"

Every syllable was audible to Burke, but Lorna was exchanging pleasantries with Shepard, who had taken Baxter's seat.

"All right, Jimmie. Beat it yourself."

Baxter turned around as Jimmie quietly slipped away. Baxter leaned over the table to smirk into the face of the young girl.

"Say, Miss Lorna, some of my friends are over in another corner of the room, and I'm going to speak to them. Now, save the next tango for me. Mr. Shepard will fix it for you, and if you jolly him right you can get into his new show, 'The Girl and the Dragon,' can't she, Sam?"

"Where are you going?" exclaimed Shepard in a gruff tone. "You've got to attend to something for me to-night."

There was a brutal dominance which vibrated in his voice. Here was a desperate character, thought Burke, who was accustomed to command others; he was not the flabby weakling type, like Baxter and Craig.

"It's better for you to do it, Sam. I'll tell you later. Jimmie just tipped me off that there's a bull on the trail that's lamped me."

Burke understood the shifting of their business arrangement, but to Lorna the crook's slang was so much gibberish.

"What did you say? I can't understand such funny talk, Mr. Baxter. I guess I had too strong a cocktail, he! he!" she exclaimed. "What about a lamp?"

"That's all right, girlie," said Shepard, as Baxter walked quickly away. "Some of his friends want him to go down to the Lamb's Club, but he doesn't want to leave you. We'll have a little chat together while he is gone. I'm not very good at dancing or I'd get you to turkey trot with me."

Lorna's voice was whiny now as she responded.

"Oh, I'm feeling funny. That cocktail was too much for me.... I guess I'd better go home."

"There, there, my dear," Shepard reassured her. "You get that way for a little while, but it's all right. You'd better have a little beer—that will straighten you up."

Only by the strongest will power could Burke resist his desire to interpose now, yet the words of the men prepared him for something which it would be more important to wait for—to interfere at the dramatic moment.

"Here, waiter, a bottle of beer!" ordered Shepard.

Burke turned half way around, and, by a side-long glance, he saw Shepard pulling a small vial from his hip pocket as he sat with his back to the policeman.

"Oh, ho! So here it comes!" thought Bobbie. "I'll be ready to stand by now."

He rose and pushed back his chair. The waiter had brought the bottle with surprising alacrity, and Shepard poured out a glass for the young girl. Bobbie stood fumbling with his change as an excuse to watch. Lorna was engrossed in the bubbling foam of the beer and did not notice him.

"I guess he's afraid to do it now," thought Bobbie, as he failed to observe any suspicious move.

True, Shepard's hand passed swiftly over the glass as he handed it to the girl.

She drank it at his urging, and then suddenly her head sank forward on her breast.

Bobbie stifled his indignation with difficulty as Shepard gave an exclamation of surprise.

"My wife! She is sick! She has fainted!" cried Shepard to Burke's amazement. The man acted his part cunningly.

He had sprung to his feet as he rushed around the table to catch the toppling girl. With a quick jump to her side Bobbie had caught her by an arm, but Shepard indignantly pushed him aside.

"How dare you, sir?" he exclaimed. "Take your hands off my wife."

The man's bravado was splendid, and even the diners were impressed. Most of them laughed, for to them it was only another drunken woman, a familiar and excruciatingly funny object to most of them.

"Aw, let the goil alone," cried one red-faced man who sat with a small, heavily rouged girl of about sixteen. "Don't come between man and wife!" And he laughed with coarse appreciation of his own humor.

Shepard had lifted Lorna with his strong arms and was starting toward the door. Burke saw the entrance to the men's café on the right. He quietly walked into it, and then hurried toward the front, out through the big glass door to the street.

There, about twenty feet to his right, he saw the purring taxicab which he had ordered waiting for a quick run.

In front of the restaurant entrance, now to his left, was another car, with a chauffeur standing by its open door, expectantly.

Burke ran up just as Shepard emerged from the restaurant entrance. The officer sprang at the big fellow and dealt him a terrible blow on the side of the head. The man staggered and his hold weakened. As he did so Burke caught the inanimate form of the young girl in his own arms. He turned before Shepard or the waiting chauffeur could recover from their surprise and ran toward the car at the right. The two men were after him, but Burke lifted the girl into the machine and cried to the chauffeur:

"Go it!"

"Who are you?"

"I'm Mr. Green," said Burke. The chauffeur sprang into his seat, but as he did so Shepard was upon the young officer and trying to climb into the door.

Biff!

Here was a chance for every ounce of accumulated ire to assert itself, and it did so, through the hardened muscles of Officer 4434's right arm. Shepard sank backward with a groan, as the taxi-cab shot forward obedient to its throttle.

Burke was bounced backward upon the unconscious girl, but the machine sped swiftly with a wise chauffeur at its wheel. He did not know where his passenger wished to go, but his judgment told him it was away from pursuit.

He turned swiftly down the first street to the right.

Back on the sidewalk before the restaurant there was intense excitement. Baxter, Craig and Jimmie the Monk had followed the artful Shepard to the street by the side door. They assisted the chauffeur in picking up the bepummeled man from the sidewalk.

"Say, Jimmie! There's somebody shadowing us. Get into that cab of Mike's and we'll chase him!" cried Baxter.

They rushed for the other cab, leaving Craig to mop Shepard's wan face with a perfumed handkerchief.

After the slight delay of cranking it the second car whizzed along the street. But that delay was fatal to the purpose of the pursuers, for ere they had reached the corner down which the first machine had turned the entire block was empty. Burke's driver had made another right turn.

Bobbie opened the door and yelled to the chauffeur as he hung to the jamb with difficulty.

"Drive past the restaurant again very slowly, but don't stop. Then keep on going straight up the avenue."

The chauffeur knew the advantage of doubling on a trail, and by the time he had passed the restaurant after a third and fourth right turn—making a trip completely around the block—the excitement had died down. The pursuers had gone on a wild-goose chase in the opposite direction, little suspecting such a simple trick.

The taxicab rumbled nonchalantly up the avenue for five or six blocks, while Burke worked in a vain effort to restore his fair prisoner to consciousness.

The car stopped in a dark stretch between blocks.

"Where shall I go, governor?" asked the chauffeur as he jumped down and opened the door. "Is your lady friend any better, governor?"

Burke looked at the man's face as well as he could in the dim light, wondering if he could be trusted. He decided that it was too big a chance, for there is a secret fraternity among chauffeurs and the denizens of the Tenderloin which is more powerful than any benevolent order ever founded. This man would undoubtedly tell of his destination to some other driver, surely to the starter at the restaurant. Then it would be a comparatively simple matter for Baxter and Jimmie the Monk to learn the details in enough fullness to track his own identity. For certain reasons, already formulated, Bobbie Burke wished to keep Jimmie and his gangsters in blissful ignorance of his own knowledge of their activities.

"This is my girl, and one of those fellows tried to steal her," said Burke in a gruff voice. "I was onto the game, and that's why I had the starter get you ready. She lives on West Seventy-first Street, near West End Avenue. Now, you run along on the right side of the street, and I'll point out the house."

He was planning a second "double" on his trail. The chauffeur grunted and started the machine again. The girl was moaning with pain in an incoherent way.

As they rolled slowly down West Seventy-first Street Bobbie saw a house which showed a light in the third floor. Presumably the storm door would not be locked, as it would have been in case the tenants were away. He knocked on the window.

The taxi came to a stop.

The chauffeur opened the door and Burke sprang out.

"Here's a ten-dollar bill, my boy," said Burke. "I'll have to square her with her mother, so you come back here in twenty minutes and take me down to that restaurant. I'm going to clean out that joint, and I'll pay you another ten to help me. Are you game?"

The chauffeur laughed wisely.

"Am I game? Just watch me."

Burke lifted Lorna out and turned toward the steps.

"Now, don't leave me in the lurch. Be back in exactly twenty minutes, and I'll be on the job—and we'll make it some job. But, don't let the folks see you standing around, or they'll think I've been up to some game. Her old man will start some shooting. Come back for me."

The chauffeur chuckled as he climbed into his car and drove away, planning a little himself.

"Any guy that has a girl as swell as that one to live on this street will be good for a hundred dollars before I get through with him," he muttered as he took a chew of tobacco. "And I've got the number of that house, too. Her old man will give a good deal to keep this out of the papers. I know my business, even if I didn't go to college!"

As the chauffeur disappeared around the corner, after taking a look toward the steps up which Burke had carried his unconscious burden, the policeman put Lorna down inside the vestibule.

"Now, this is a dangerous game. It means disgrace if I get caught; but it means a pair of broken hearts if this poor girl gets caught," he thought. "I'll risk nobody coming, and run for another taxi."

He hastened down the steps and walked around the corner, hurrying toward a big hotel which stood not far from Broadway. Here he found another taxicab.

"There's a young lady sick at the house of one of my friends, and I'm taking her home," said Burke to the driver. "Hurry up, please."

The second automobile sped over the street to the house where Burke had left the girl, and the officer hurried up the steps. He soon reappeared with Lorna in his arms, walked calmly down the steps, and put her into the car.

This time he gave the correct home address, and the taxicab rumbled along on the last stretch of the race.

They passed the first car, whose driver was already planning the ways to spend the money which he was to make by a little scientific blackmail.

He was destined to a long wait in front of the brownstone mansion.

After nearly an hour he decided to take things into his own hands.

"I'll get a little now," he muttered with an accompaniment of profanity. "That guy can't stall me."

After ringing the bell for several minutes a very angry caretaker came to the door.

"What do you want, my man?" cried this individual in unmistakable British accents. "Dash your blooming impudence in waking me up at this time in the morning."

"I want to get my taxicab fare from the gent that brought the lady here drunk!" declared the chauffeur. "Are you her father?"

The caretaker shook a fist in his face as he snapped back:

"I'm nobody's father. There ain't no gent nor drunk lady here. I'm alone in this house, and my master and missus is at Palm Beach. If you don't get away from here I'm going to call the police."

With that he slammed the door in the face of the astounded chauffeur and turned out the light in the hall.

The taxi driver walked down the steps slowly.

"Well, that's a new game on me!" he grunted. "There's a new gang working this town as sure as I'm alive. I'm going down and put the starter wise."

Down he went, to face a cross-examination from the starter, and an accounting for his time. He had to pay over seven dollars of his ten to cover the period for which he had the car out. Jimmie the Monk and Baxter had returned from their unsuccessful chase. As they made their inquiries from the starter and learned the care with which the coup d'état had been arranged they lapsed into angry, if admiring, profanity.

"Some guy, eh, Jimmie!" exclaimed Baxter. "But we'll find out who it was, all right. Leave it to me!"

"Say, dat bloke was crazy—crazy like a fox, wasn't he?" answered Jimmie. "He let Shepard do de deal, and den he steals de kitty! Dis is what I calls cut-throat competition!"

CHAPTER VII

THE CLOSER BOND

Once in the second taxicab Burke's difficulties were not at an end.

"I want to get this poor young girl home without humiliating her or her family, if I can," was his mental resolve. "But I can't quite plan it. I wish I could take her to Dr. MacFarland, but his office is 'way downtown from here."

When the car drew up before the door of Lorna's home, from which she had departed in such blithe spirits, Bob's heart was thumping almost guiltily. He felt in some ridiculous way as though he were almost responsible for her plight himself. Perhaps he had done wrong to wait so long. Yet, even his quick eyesight had failed to discover the knockout drops or powder which the wily Shepard had slipped into that disastrous glass of beer. Maybe his interference would have saved her from this unconscious stupor, indeed, he felt morally certain that it would; but Bob knew in his heart that the clever tricksters would have turned the tables on him effectively, and undoubtedly in the end would have won their point by eluding him and escaping with the girl. It was better that their operations should be thwarted in a manner which would prevent them from knowing how sharply they were watched. Bob knew that these men were to be looked after in the future.

He cast aside his thoughts to substitute action.

"Here's your number, mister," said the chauffeur, who opened the door. "Can I help you with the lady?"

"Thank you, no. What's the charge?"

The driver twisted the lamp around to show the meter, and Burke paid him a good tip over the price of the ride.

"Shall I wait for you?" asked the driver.

"No; that's all. I'll walk to the subway as soon as my friend gets in. Good night."

The chauffeur lingered a bit as Bob took the girl in his arms. The officer understood the suggestion of his hesitation.

"I said good night!" he spoke curtly.

The taxi man understood this time; there was no mistaking the firmness of the hint, and he started his machine away.

The Bartons lived in one of the apartments of the building. The front door was locked, and so Bob was forced reluctantly to ring the bell beneath the name which indicated their particular letter box.

He waited, holding the young girl in his arms.

"Oh, I'm so sick!" he heard her say faintly, and he realized that she was regaining consciousness.

"If only I can get her upstairs quietly," he thought.

He was about to swing her body around in his arms so that he could ring once more when there was a turning of the knob.

"Who is it?" came a frightened voice.

It was Mary Barton at the doorway.

"S-s-s-h!" cautioned Bob. "It's Burke. I'm bringing Miss Lorna home? Don't make any noise."

"Oh!" gasped the unhappy sister. "What's wrong? Is she hurt?"

"No!" said Bob. "Fortunately not."

"Is she— Oh— Is she—drunk?"

Burke calmed her with the reassurance of his low, steady voice.

"No, Miss Mary. She was drugged by those rascals, and I saved her in time. Please don't cry, or make a noise. Let me take her upstairs and help you. It's better if she does not know that I was the one to bring her home."

Mary tried to help him; but Bob carried the girl on into the hall.

"Is your father awake?"

"No; I told him two hours ago, when he asked me from his room, that Lorna had returned and was asleep. He believed me. I had to fib to save him from breaking his dear old daddy heart. Is she injured at all?"

It was plainly evident that the poor girl was holding her nerves in leash with a tremendous effort.

Bob kept on toward the stairs.

"She'll be all right when you get her into her room. Give her some smelling salts, and don't tell your father. Didn't he hear the bell?"

"No; I've been waiting for her. I put some paper in the bell so that it would only buzz when it rang. Let me help you, Mr. Burke. How on earth did you——" She was eager in spite of her anxiety.

To see the young officer returning with her sister this way was more of a mystery than she could fathom. But, at Bob's sibilant command for silence, she trustingly obeyed, and went up before him to guide the way along the darkened stairway.

At last they reached the door of their apartment.

Mary opened it, and Bob entered, walking softly. She led the way to her humble little bedroom, the one which she and Lorna shared. Bob laid the sister upon the bed, and beckoned Mary to follow him. Lorna was moving now, her hands tremulous, and she was half-moaning.

"I want my Mary. I want my Mary."

Her sister followed Burke out into the hall, which led down the steps to the street.

"Now, remember, don't tell her about being drugged. A man at one of the tables put some knockout drops into a glass of water"—Bob was softening the blow with a little honest lying—"and I rescued her just in time. She knows nothing about it—only warn her about the company that she was in. I have learned that they are worse than worthless. I will attend to them in my own way, and in the line of my work, Miss Mary. But, as you love your sister, don't ever let her go with those men again."

Mary's hand was outstretched toward the young man's, and he took it gently.

"You've done much for Lorna," she breathed softly, "and more for me!"

There was a sweet pressure from those soft, clasping fingers which thrilled Bob as though somehow he was burying his face in a bunch of roses—like that first one which had tapped its soft message for admission to his heart, back in the hospital.

"Good night. Don't worry. It's all ended well, after all."

Mary drew away her fingers reluctantly as he backed down one step.

"Good night—Bob!"

That was all. She slipped quietly inside the apartment and closed the door noiselessly behind her.

Bob slowly descended the steps; oddly enough, he felt as though it were an ascension of some sort. His life seemed to be going into higher planes, and his hopes and ambitions came fluttering into his brain like the shower of petals from some blossom-laden tree. He felt anew the spring of old dreams, and the surge of new ones.

He stumbled, unsteady in his steps, his hands trembling on the railing of the stairs, until he reached the street level. He hurried out through the hallway and closed the door behind him.

How he longed to retrace his steps for just one more word! That first tender use of his name had a wealth of meaning which stirred him more than a torrent of endearing terms.

The keen bracing air of the early spring morning thrilled him.

He hurried down the street toward the subway station, elated, exalted.

"It's worth fighting every gangster in New York for a girl like her!" he told himself. "I never realized how bitter all this was until it struck home to me— by striking home to some one who is loved by the girl—I love."

The trip downtown was more tiring than he had expected. The stimulus of his exciting evening was now wearing off, and Bob went direct to the station house to be handy for the duty which began early in the day. It was not yet dawn, but the rattling milk carts, the stirring of trucks and the early stragglers of morning workers gave evidence that the sun would soon be out upon his daily travels.

The day passed without more excitement than usual. Bob took his turn after a short nap in the dormitory room of the station house. During his relief he rested up again. When he was preparing to start out again upon patrol a letter was handed him by the captain.

"Here, Burke, a little message from your best girl, I suppose," smiled his superior.

Bob took it, and as he opened it again he felt that curious thrill which had been aroused in him by the winsome charm of Mary Barton. It was a brief note which she had mailed that morning on her way to work.

"DEAR MR. BURKE—Everything was all right after all our worry. Lorna is heartily repentant, and thinks that she had to be brought home by one of her 'friends' (?). She has promised never to go with them again, and, aside from a bad headache to-day, she is no worse for her folly. Father knows nothing, and, dear soul, I feel that it is better so. I can never thank you enough. I hope to see you soon.

"Cordially,
"MARY."

Bob folded the note and tucked it into his breast pocket. The captain had been watching him with shrewd interest, and presently he intercepted: "Ah, now, I guessed right. Why, Bobbie Burke, you're even blushing like a schoolgirl over her first beau."

Burke was just a trifle resentful under the sharp look of the captain's gray eyes; but the unmistakable friendliness of the officer's face drove away all feeling.

"I envy you, my boy. I am not making fun of you," said the captain, with keen understanding.

"Thank you, Cap," said Bob quietly. "You guessed right both times. It's my first sweetheart."

He buttoned his coat and started for the door.

"You'd better step around to Doc MacFarland's on your rounds this evening and let him look you over. It won't take but a minute, and I don't expect him around the station. You're not on peg-post to-night, so you can do it."

"All right, Cap."

Burke saluted and left the station, falling into line with the other men who were marching out on relief.

A half hour later he dropped into the office of the police surgeon, and was greeted warmly by the old gentleman.

MacFarland was smoking his pipe in comfort after the cares and worries of a busy day.

"Any more trouble with the gangsters, Burke?" he asked.

Bob, after a little hesitation decided to tell him about the adventure of the night before.

"I want your advice, Doc, for you understand these things. Do you suppose there's any danger of Lorna's going out with those fellows again? You don't suppose that they were actually going to entice her into some house, do you?"

MacFarland stroked his gray whiskers.

"Well, my boy, that is not what we Scotchmen would call a vera canny thought! You speak foolishly. Why, don't you know that is organized teamwork just as fine as they make it? Those two fellows, Baxter, I think you said, and Craig, are typical 'cadets.' They are the pretty boys who make the acquaintance of the girls, and open the way for temptation, which is generally attended to by other men of stronger caliber. This fellow Shepard is undoubtedly one of the head men of their gang. If Jimmie the Monk is mixed up in it that is the connecting link between these fellows and the East Side. And it's back to the East Side that the trail nearly always leads, for over in the East Side of New York is the feudal fastness of the politician who tells the public to be damned, and is rewarded with a fortune for his pains. The politician protects the gangster; the gangster protects the procurer, and both of them vote early and often for the politician."

Bob sighed.

"Isn't there some way that this young girl can be warned about the dangers she is running into? It's terrible to think of a thing like this threatening any girl of good family, or any other family for that matter."

"You must simply warn her sister and have her watch the younger girl like a hawk."

MacFarland cleaned out his pipe with a scalpel knife, and put in another charge of tobacco.

He puffed a blue cloud before Bob had replied.

"I wish there were some way I could get co-operation on this. I'm going to hunt these fellows down, Doc. But it seems to me that the authorities in this city should help along."

"They are helping along. The District Attorney has sent up gangster after gangster; but it's like a quicksand, Burke—new rascals seem to slide in as fast as you shovel out the old ones."

"I have the advantage now that they don't know who is looking after Lorna," said Bobbie. "But it was a hard job getting them off my track."

"That was good detective work—as good as I've heard of," said the doctor. "You just keep shy now. Don't get into more gun fights and fist scraps for a few days, and you'll get something on them again. You know your catching them last night was just part of a general law about crime. The criminal always gives himself away in some little, careless manner that hardly looks worth while worrying about. Those two fellows never dreamed of your following them—they let the name of the restaurant slip out, and probably forgot about it the next minute. And Jimmie the Monk has given you a clue to work on, to find out the connection. Keep up your work—but keep a bullet-proof skin for a while."

Bob started toward the door. A new idea came to him.

"Doctor, I've just thought of something. I saw a picture in the paper to-night of a big philanthropist named Trubus, or something like that, who is fighting Raines Law Hotels, improper novels, bad moving pictures and improving morals in general. How do you think it would do to give him a tip about these fellows? He asks for more money from the public to carry on their work. They had a big banquet in his honor last night."

MacFarland laughed, and took from his desk a letter, which he handed to Bob with a wink. The young officer was surprised, but took the paper, and glanced at it.

"There, Burke, read this letter. If I get one of these a day, I get five, all in the same tune. Isn't that enough to make a man die a miser?"

Officer 4434 took the letter over to the doctor's student lamp and read with amusement:

"DEAR SIR—The Purity League is waging the great battle against sin.

"You are doubtless aware that in this glorious work it is necessary for us to defray office and other expenses. Whatever tithe of your blessings can be donated to our Rescue Fund will be bread cast upon the waters to return tenfold.

"A poor widow, whose only child is a beautiful girl of seventeen, has been taken under the care of our gentle nurses. This unfortunate woman, a devout church attendant, has been prostrated by the wanton conduct of her daughter, who has left the influence of home to enter upon a life of wickedness.

"If you will contribute one hundred dollars to the support of this miserable old creature, we will have collected enough to pay her a pension from the interest of the fund of ten dollars monthly. Upon receipt of your check for this amount we will send you, express prepaid, a framed membership certificate, richly embossed in gold, and signed by the President, Treasurer and Chaplain-Secretary of the Purity League. Your name will be entered upon our roster as a patron of the organization.

"Make all checks payable to William Trubus, President, and on out-of-town checks kindly add clearing-house fee.

"'Charity shall cover the multitude of sins.'"—I Peter, iv. 8.

"Yours for the glory of the Cause,
"WILLIAM TRUBUS,
"President, The Purity League of N. Y."

As Officer Burke finished the letter he looked quizzically at Dr. MacFarland.

"How large was your check, doctor?"

"My boy, I came from Scotland. I will give you three guesses."

"But, doctor, I see the top of the letter-head festooned with about twenty-five names, all of them millionaires. Why don't these men contribute the money direct? Then they could save the postage. This letter is printed, not typewritten. They must have sent out thousands about this poor old woman. Surely some millionaire could give up one monkey dinner and endow the old lady?"

"Burke, you're young in the ways of charity. That old woman is an endowment herself. She ought to bring enough royalties for the Purity League to buy three new mahogany desks, hire five new investigators and four extra stenographers."

The old doctor's kindly face lost its geniality as he pounded on the table with rising ire.

"Burke, I have looked into this organized charity game. It is a disgrace. Out of every hundred dollars given to a really worthy cause, in answer to hundreds of thousands of letters, ninety dollars go to office and executive expenses. When a poor man or a starving woman finally yields to circumstances and applies to one of these richly-endowed institutions, do you know what happens?"

Burke shook his head.

"The object of divine assistance enters a room, which has nice oak benches down either side. She, and most of them are women (for men have a chance to panhandle, and consider it more self-respecting to beg on the streets than from a religious corporation), waits her turn, until a dizzy blonde clerk beckons condescendingly. She advances to the rail, and gives her name, race, color, previous condition of servitude, her mother's great grandmother's maiden name, and a lot of other important charitable things. She is then referred to room six hundred and ninety. There she gives more of her autobiography. From this room she is sent to the inspection department, and she is investigated further. If the poor woman doesn't faint from hunger and exhaustion she keeps up this schedule until she has walked a Marathon around the fine white marble building devoted to charity. At last she gets a ticket for a meal, or a sort of trading stamp by which she can get a room for the night in a vermin-infested lodging house, upon the additional payment of thirty cents. Now, this may seem exaggerated, but honestly, my boy, I have given you just about the course of action of these scientific philanthropic enterprises. They are spic and span as the quarterdeck of a millionaire's yacht."

MacFarland was so disgusted with the objects of his tirade that he tried three times before he could fill his old briar pipe.

"Doctor, why don't you air these opinions where they will count?" asked Bobbie. "It's time to stop the graft."

"When some newspaper is brave enough to risk the enmity of church people, who don't know real conditions, and thus lose a few subscribers, or when some really charitable people investigate for themselves, it will all come out. The real truth of that quotation at the bottom of the Purity League letter should be expressed this way: 'Charity covers a multitude of hypocrites and grafters.' And to my mind the dirtiest, foulest, lowest grafter in the world is the man who does it under the cloak of charity or religion. But a man who proclaims such a belief as mine is called an atheist and a destroyer of ideals."

Burke looked at the old doctor admiringly.

"If there were more men like you, Doc, there wouldn't be so much hypocrisy, and there would be more real good done. Anyhow, I believe I'll look up this angelic Trubus to see what he's like."

He took up his night stick and started for the door.

"I've spent too much time in here, even if it was at the captain's orders. Now I'll go out and earn what the citizens think is the easy money of a policeman. Good night."

"Good night, my lad. Mind what I told you, and don't let those East Side goblins get you."

Burke had a busy night.

He had hardly been out of the house before he heard a terrific explosion a block away, and he ran to learn the cause.

From crowded tenement houses came swarming an excited, terror-stricken stream of tenants. The front of a small Italian store had been smashed in. It was undoubtedly the work of a bomb, and already the cheap structure of the building had caught the flames. Men and women, children by the dozen, all screeched and howled in a Babel of half a dozen languages as Bob, with his fellow officers, tried to calm them.

The engines were soon at the scene, but not until Bob and others had dashed into the burning building half a dozen times to guide the frightened occupants to the streets.

Mothers would remember that babies had been left inside—after they themselves had been brought to safety. The long-suffering policemen would rush back to get the little ones.

The fathers of these aliens seemed to forget family ties, and even that chivalry, supposed to be a masculine instinct, for they fought with fist and foot to get to safety, regardless of their women and the children. The reserves from the station had to be called out to keep the fire lines intact, while the grimy firemen worked with might and main to keep the blaze from spreading. After it was all over Burke wondered whether these great hordes of aliens were of such benefit to the country as their political compatriots avowed. He had been reading long articles in the newspapers denouncing Senators and Representatives who wished to restrict immigration. He had seen glowing accounts of the value of strong workers for the development of the country's enterprise, of the duty of Americans to open their national portal to the down-trodden of other lands, no matter how ignorant or poverty-stricken.

"I believe much of this vice and crime comes from letting this rabble into the city, where they stay, instead of going out into the country where they can work and get fresh air and fields. They take the jobs of honest men, who are Americans, and I see by the papers that there are two hundred and fifty thousand men out of work and hunting jobs in New York this spring," mused Bob. "It appears to me as if we might look after Americans first for a while, instead of letting in more scum. Cheap labor is all right; but when honest men have to pay higher taxes to take care of the peasants of Europe who don't want to work, and who do crowd our hospitals and streets, and fill our schools with their children, and our jails and hospitals with their work and their diseases, it's a high price for cheap labor."

And, without knowing it, Officer 4434 echoed the sentiments of a great many of his fellow citizens who are not catering to the votes of foreign-born constituents or making fortunes from the prostitution of workers' brain and brawn.

The big steamship companies, the cheap factory proprietors and the great merchants who sell the sweat-shop goods at high-art prices, the manipulators of subway and road graft, the political jobbers, the anarchistic and socialistic sycophants of class guerilla warfare are continually arguing to the contrary. But the policemen and the firemen of New York City can tell a different story of the value of our alien population of more than two million!

CHAPTER VIII

THE PURITY LEAGUE AND ITS ANGEL

In a few days, when an afternoon's relief allowed him the time, Officer 4434 decided to visit the renowned William Trubus. He found the address of that patron of organized philanthropy in the telephone book at the station house.

It was on Fifth Avenue, not far from the windswept coast of the famous Flatiron Building.

Burke started up to the building shortly before one o'clock, and he found it difficult to make his way along the sidewalks of the beautiful avenue because of the hordes of men and girls who loitered about, enjoying the last minutes of their luncheon hour.

Where a few years before had been handsome and prosperous shops, with a throng of fashionably dressed pedestrians of the city's better classes on the sidewalks, the district had been taken over by shirtwaist and cloak factories. The ill-fed, foul-smelling foreigners jabbered in their native dialects, ogled the gum-chewing girls and grudgingly gave passage-way to the young officer, who, as usual, when off duty, wore his civilian clothes.

"I wonder why these factories don't use the side streets instead of spoiling the finest avenue in America?" thought Bob. "I guess it is because the foreigners of their class spoil everything they seem to touch. Our great granddaddies fought for Liberty, and now we have to give it up and pay for the privilege!"

It was with a pessimistic thought like this that he entered the big office structure in which was located the headquarters of the Purity League. Bob took the elevator in any but a happy frame of mind. He was determined to find out for himself just how correct was Dr. MacFarland's estimate of high-finance-philanthropy.

On the fourth floor he left the car, and entered the door which bore the name of the organization.

A young girl, toying with the wires of a telephone switchboard, did not bother to look up, despite his query.

"Yes, dearie," she confided to some one at the other end of the telephone. "We had the grandest time. He's a swell feller, all right, and opened nothing but wine all evening. Yes, I had my charmeuse gown—the one with the pannier, you know, and——"

"Excuse me," interrupted Burke, "I'd like to speak to the president of this company."

The girl looked at him scornfully.

"Just a minute, girlie, I'm interrupted." She turned to look at Bob again, and with a haughty toss of her rather startling yellow curls raised her eyebrows in a supercilious glance of interrogation.

"What's your business?"

"That's *my* business. I want to see Mr. Trubus and not *you*."

"Well, nix on the sarcasm. He's too busy to be disturbed by every book agent and insurance peddler in town. Tell me what you want and I'll see if it's important enough. That's what I'm paid for."

"You tell him that a policeman from the —— precinct wants to see him, and tell him mighty quick!" snapped Burke with a sharp look.

He expected a change of attitude. But the curious, shifty look in the girl's face—almost a pallor which overspread its artificial carnadine, was inexplicable to him at this time. He had cause to remember it later.

"Why, why," she half stammered, "what's the matter?"

"You give him my message."

The girl did not telephone as Burke had expected her to do, according to the general custom where switchboard girls send in announcement of callers to private offices.

Instead she removed the headgear of the receiver and rose. She went inside the door at her back and closed it after her.

"Well, that's some service," thought Burke. "I wonder why she's so active after indifference?"

She returned before he had a chance to ruminate further.

"You can go right in, sir," she said.

As she sat down she watched him from the corner of her eye. Burke could not help but wonder at the tense interest in his presence, but dismissed the thought as he entered the room, and beheld the president of the Purity League.

William Trubus was seated at a broad mahogany desk, while before him was spread a large, old-fashioned family Bible. He held in his left hand a cracker, which he was munching daintily, as he read in an abstracted manner from the page before him. In his right hand was a glass containing a red liquid, which Burke at first sight supposed was wine. He was soon to be undeceived.

He stood a full minute while the president of the League mumbled to himself as he perused the Sacred Writ. Bobbie was thus enabled to get a clear view of the philanthropist's profile, and to study the great man from a good point of vantage.

Trubus was rotund. His cheeks were rosy evidences of good health, good meals and freedom from anxiety as to where those good meals were to come from. His forehead was round, and being partially bald, gave an appearance of exaggerated intellectuality.

His nose was that of a Roman centurion—bold, cruel as a hawk's beak, strong-nostriled as a wolf's muzzle. His firm white teeth, as they crunched on the cracker suggested, even stronger, the semblance to a carnivorous animal of prey. A benevolent-looking pair of gold-rimmed glasses sat astride that nose, but Burke noticed that, oddly enough, Trubus did not need them for his reading, nor later when he turned to look at the young officer.

The plump face was adorned with the conventional "mutton-chop" whiskers which are so generally associated in one's mental picture of bankers, bishops and reformers. The whiskers were so resolutely black, that Burke felt sure they must have been dyed, for Trubus' plump hands, with their wrinkles and yellow blotches, evidenced that the philanthropist must have passed the three-score milestone of time.

The white gaiters, the somber black of his well-fitting broadcloth coat of ministerial cut, the sanctified, studied manner of the man's pose gave Burke an almost indefinable feeling that before him sat a cleverly "made-up" actor, not a sincere, natural man of benevolent activities.

The room was furnished elaborately; some rare Japanese ivories adorned the desk top. A Chinese vase, close by, was filled with fresh-cut flowers. Around the walls were handsome oil paintings. Beautiful Oriental rugs covered the floor. There hung a tapestry from some old French convent; yonder stood an exquisite marble statue whose value must have been enormous.

As Trubus raised the glass to drink the red liquid Bobbie caught the glint of an enormous diamond ring which must have cost thousands.

"Well, evidently his charity begins at home!" thought the young man as he stepped toward the desk.

Tiring of the wait he addressed the absorbed reader.

"I beg your pardon, Mr. Trubus, but I was announced and told to come in here to see you."

Trubus raised his eyebrows, and slowly turned in his chair. His eyes opened wide with surprise as he peered over the gold rims at the newcomer.

"Well, well, well! So you were, so you were."

He put down his glass reluctantly.

"You must pardon me, but I always spend my noon hour gaining inspiration from the great Source of all inspiration. What can I do for you? I understand that you are a policeman—am I mistaken?"

"No, sir; I am a policeman, and I have come to you to get your aid. I understand that you receive a great deal of money for your campaign for purifying the city, and so I think you can help me in a certain work."

Trubus waved the four-carat ring deprecatingly.

"Ah, my young friend, you are in great error. I do not receive much money. We toil very ardently for the cause, but worldly pleasures and the selfishness of our fellow citizens interfere with our solving of the great task. We are far behind in our receipts. How lamentably little do we get in response to our requests for aid to charity!"

He followed Bobbie's incredulous glance at the luxurious furnishings of his office.

"Yes, yes, it is indeed a wretched state of affairs. Our efforts never cease, and although we have fourteen stenographers working constantly on the lists of people who could aid us, with a number of devout assistants who cover the field, our results are pitiable."

He leaned back in his leather-covered mahogany desk chair.

"Even I, the president of this association, give all my time to the cause. And for what? A few hundred dollars yearly—a bare modicum. I am compelled to eat this frugal luncheon of crackers and grape juice. I have given practically all of my private fortune to this splendid enterprise, and the results are discouraging. Even the furniture of this office I have brought down from my home in order that those who may come to discuss our movement may be surrounded by an environment of beauty and calm. But, money, much money. Alas!"

Just at this juncture the door opened and the telephone girl brought in a basket full of letters, evidently just received from the mail man.

"Here's the latest mail, Mr. Trubus. All answers to the form letters, to judge from the return envelopes."

Trubus frowned at her as he caught Burke's twinkling glance.

"Doubtless they are insults to our cause, not replies to our importunities, Miss Emerson!" he hurriedly replied.

He looked sharply at Burke.

"Well, sir, having finished what I consider my midday devotions, I am very busy. What can I do for you?"

"You can listen to what I have to say," retorted Burke; resenting the condescending tone. "I come here to see you about some actual conditions. I have read some of your literature, and if you are as anxious to do some active good as you write you are, I can give you enough to keep your entire organization busy."

It was a very different personality which shone forth from those sharp black eyes now, than the smug, quasi-religious man who had spoken before.

"I don't like your manner, young man. Tell me what you have to say, and do it quickly."

"Well, yours is the Purity League. I happen to have run across a gang of procurers who drug girls, and make their livelihood off the shame of the girls they get into their clutches. I can give you the names of these men, their haunts, and you can apply the funds and influence of your society in running them to earth, with my assistance and that of a number of other policemen I know."

Trubus rose from his chair.

"I have heard this story many times before, my young friend. It does not interest me."

"What!" exclaimed Burke, "you advertise and obtain money from the public to fight for purity and when a man comes to you with facts and with the gameness to help you fight, you say you are not interested."

Trubus waved his hand toward the door by which Burke had entered.

"I have to make an address to our Board of Directors this afternoon," he said, "and I don't care to associate my activities nor those of the cause for which I stand with the police department. You had better carry your information to your superiors."

"But, I tell you I have the leads which will land a gang of organized procurers, if you will give me any of your help. The police are trying to do the best they can, but they have to fight district politics, saloon men, and every sort of pull against justice. Your society isn't afraid of losing its job, and it can't be fired by political influence. Why don't you spend some of your money for the cause that's alive instead of on furniture and stenographers and diamond rings!"

The cat was out of the bag.

Trubus brought his fist down with a bang which spilled grape juice on his neat piles of papers.

"Don't you dictate to me. You police are a lot of grafters, in league with the gangsters and the politicians. My society cares for the unfortunate and seeks to work its reforms by mentally and spiritually uplifting the poor. We have the support of the clergy and those people who know that the public and the poor must be brought to a spiritual understanding. Pah! Don't come around to me with your story of 'organized traffic.' That's one of the stories originated by the police to excuse their inefficiency!"

Burke's eyes flamed as he stood his ground.

"Let me tell you, Mr. Trubus, that before you and your clergy can do any good with people's souls you've got to take more care of their bodies. You've got to clean out some of the rotten tenement houses which some of your big churches own. I've seen them—breeding places for tuberculosis and drunkenness, and crime of the vilest sort. You've got to give work to the thousands of starving men and women, who are driven to crime, instead of spending millions on cathedrals and altars and statues and stained glass windows, for people who come to church in their automobiles. A lot of your churches are closed up when the neighborhood changes and only poor people attend. They sell the property to a saloonkeeper, or turn it into a moving-picture house and burn people to death in the rotten old fire-trap. And if you don't raise your hand, when I come to you fair and square, with an honest story—if you dare to order me out of here, because you've got to gab a lot of your charity drivel to a board of directors, instead of taking the interest any real man would take in something that was real and vital and eating into the very heart of New York life, I'm going to show you up, and put you out of the charity business——so help me God!"

Burke's right arm shot into the air, with the vow, and his fist clenched until the knuckles stood out ridged against the bloodless pallor of his tense skin.

Trubus looked straight into Burke's eyes, and his own gaze dropped before the white flame which was burning in them.

Burke turned without a word and walked from the office.

After he had gone Trubus rang the buzzer for his telephone girl.

"Miss Emerson, did that policeman leave his name and station?"

"No, sir; but I know his number. He's mighty fresh."

"Well, I must find out who he is. He is a dangerous man."

Trubus turned toward his mail, and with a slight tremor in his hand which the shrewd girl noticed began to open the letters.

Check after check fluttered to the surface of the desk, and the great philanthropist regained his composure by degrees. When he had collected the postage offertory, carefully indorsed them all, and assembled the funds sent in for his great work, he slipped them into a generously roomy wallet, and placed the latter in the pocket of his frock coat.

He opened a drawer in his desk, and drew forth a tan leather bank book. Taking his silk hat from the bronze hook by the door, he closed the desk, after slamming the Bible shut with a sacrilegious impatience, quite out of keeping with his manner of a half hour earlier.

"I am going to the bank, Miss Emerson. I will return in half an hour to lead in the prayer at the opening of the directors' meeting. Kindly inform the gentlemen when they arrive."

He slammed the door as he left the offices.

The telephone operator abstractedly chewed her gum as she watched his departure.

"I wonder now. I ain't seen his nibs so flustered since I been on this job," she mused. "That cop must 'ave got his goat. I wonder!"

CHAPTER IX

THE BUSY MART OF TRADE

The hypocrisy of William Trubus and the silly fatuity of his reform work rankled in Burke's bosom as he betook himself uptown to enjoy his brief vacation for an afternoon with his old friend, the inventor. Later he was to share supper when the girls came home from their work.

John Barton was busy with his new machine, and had much to talk about. At last, when his own enthusiasm had partially spent itself, he noticed Burke's depression.

"What is the trouble, my boy? You are very nervous. Has anything gone wrong?"

Bobbie hesitated. He wished to avoid any mention of the case in which Lorna had so unfortunately figured. But, at last, he unfolded the story of his interview with the alleged philanthropist, describing the situation of the gangsters and their work in general terms.

Barton shook his head.

"They're nearly all alike, these reformers in mahogany chairs, Burke. I've been too busy with machinery and workmen, whom I always tried to help along, to take much stock in the reform game. But there's no denying that we do need all the reforming that every good man in the world can give us. Only, there are many ways to go about it. Even I, without much education, and buried for years in my own particular kind of rut, can see that."

"The best kind of reform will be with the night stick and the bars of Sing Sing, Mr. Barton," answered Burke. "Some day the police will work like army men, with an army man at the head of them. It won't be politics at all then, but they'll have the backing of a man who is on the firing line, instead of sipping tea in a swell hotel, or swapping yarns and other things in a political club. That day is not far distant, either, to judge from the way people are waking things up. But we need a little different kind of preaching and reforming now."

Barton leaned back in his wheel chair and spoke reminiscently.

"Last spring I spent Sunday with a well-to-do friend of mine in a beautiful little town up in Connecticut. We went to church. It was an old colonial edifice, quaint, clean, and outside on the green before it were forty or fifty automobiles, for, as my friend told me with pride, it was the richest congregation in that part of New England.

"Inside of the church was the perfume of beautiful spring flowers which decorated the altar and were placed in vases along the aisles. In the congregation were happy, well-fed, healthy business men who enlivened existence with golf, motoring, riding, good books, good music, good plays and good dinners. Their wives were charmingly gowned. Their children were rosy-cheeked, happy and normal.

"The minister, a sweet, genial old chap, recited his text after the singing of two or three beautiful hymns. It was that quotation from the Bible: 'Look at the lilies of the field. They toil not, neither do they spin.' In full, melodious tones he addressed his congregation, confident in his own faith of a delightful hereafter, and still better blessed with the knowledge that his monthly check was not subject to the rise and fall of the stock market!

"In his sermon he spoke of the beauties of life, the freshness of spring, its message of eternal happiness for those who had earned the golden reward of the Hereafter. He preached optimism, the subject of the unceasing care and love of the Father above; he told of the spiritual joy which comes only with a profound faith in the Almighty, who observes even of the fall of the sparrow.

"Through the window came the soft breezes of the spring morning, the perfume of buds on the trees and the twitter of birds. It was a sweet relief to me after having left the dreary streets of the city and our busy machine shop behind, to see the happiness, content, decency and right living shining in the faces of the people about me. The charm of the spring was in the message of the preacher, although it was in his case more like the golden light of a sunset, for he was a good old man, who had followed his own teachings, and it was evident that he was beloved by every one in his congregation. A man couldn't help loving that old parson—he was so happy and honest!

"When he completed his sermon of content, happiness and unfaltering faith, a girl sang an old-time offertory. The services were closed with the music of a well-trained choir. The congregation rose. The worshippers finally went out of the church, chatting and happy with the thought of a duty well done in their weekly worship, and, last but not least, the certainty of a generous New England dinner at home. The church services were ended. Later in the afternoon would be a short song service of vespers and in the evening a simple and sincere meeting of sweet-minded, clean-souled young men and women for prayer service. It was all very pretty.

"As I say, Burke, it was something that soothed me like beautiful music after the rotten, miserable, wretched conditions I had seen in the city. It does a fellow good once in a while to get away from the grip of the tenements, the shades of the skyscrapers, the roar of the factories, and the shuffling, tired footsteps of the crowds, the smell of the sweat-shops.

"But, do you know, it seemed to me that that minister missed something; that he was *too contented*. There was a message that man *could* have given which I think might perhaps have disagreed with the digestions of his congregation. Undoubtedly, it would have influenced the hand that wrote the check the following month.

"I wondered to myself why, at least, he could not have spoken to his flock in words something like this, accompanied by a preliminary pound on his pulpit to awaken his congregation from dreams of golf, roast chicken and new gowns:

"'You business men who sit here so happy and so contented with honorable wives, with sturdy children in whose veins run the blood of a dozen generations of decent living, do you realize that there are any other conditions in life but yours? Do you know that Henry Brown, Joe Smith and Richard Black, who work as clerks for you down in your New York office, do not have this church, do not have these spring flowers and the Sunday dinners you will have when you go back home? Does it occur to you that these young men on their slender salaries may be supporting more people back home than you are? Do you know that many of them have no club to go to except the corner saloon or the pool room? Do you know that the only exercise a lot of your poor clerks, assistants and factory workers get is standing around on the street corners, that the only drama and comedy they ever see is in a dirty, stinking, germ-infected, dismal little movie theater in the slums; that the only music they ever hear is in the back room of a Raines Law hotel or from a worn-out hurdy-gurdy?

"'Why don't you men take a little more interest in the young fellows who work for you or in some of the old ones with dismal pasts and worse futures? Why don't you well-dressed women take an interest in the stenographers and shop girls, the garment-makers—*not* to condescend and offer them tracts and abstracts of the Scriptures—but to improve the moral conditions under which they work, the sanitary conditions, and to arrange decent places for them to amuse themselves after hours.

"'Surely you can spare a little time from the Golf Clubs and University Clubs and Literary Clubs and Bridge Clubs and Tango Parties. Let me tell you that if you do not, during the next five or ten years, the people of these classes will imbibe still more to the detriment of our race, the anarchy and money lust which is being preached to them daily, nightly and almost hourly by the socialists, the anarchists and the atheists, who are all soured on life because they've never *had* it!

"'The tide of social unrest is sweeping across to us from the Old World which will engulf our civilization unless it is stopped by the jetties of social assistance and the breakwaters of increased moral education. You can't do this with Sunday-school papers and texts! You can't stem the movement in your clubs by denouncing the demagogues over highball glasses and teacups.

"'It is all right to have faith in the good. It is well to have hope for the future. Charity is essential to right living and right helping. But out of the five million people in New York City, four million and a half have never seen any evidence of Divine assistance such as our Good Book says is given to the sparrow. They are not lilies of the field. They must toil or die. You people are to them the lilies of the field! Your fine gowns, your happy lives, your endless opportunities for amusement; your extravagances are to them as the matador's flag to the bull in the Spanish ring. Unless you *do* take the interest, unless you *do* fight to stem the movement of these dwarfed and bitter leaders, unless you *do* overcome their arguments based on much solid-rock truth by definite personal work, by definite constructive education, your civilization, my civilization and the civilization of all the centuries will fall before socialism and anarchy.'

"But *that* was not what he said. I have never heard the minister of a rich congregation say that yet. Have you, Burke?"

"No, the minister who talked like that would have to look for a new pulpit, or get a job as a carpenter, like the Minister long ago, who made the rich men angry. But I had no idea that you thought about such things, Mr. Barton. You'd make a pretty good minister yourself."

The old inventor laughed as he patted the young man on the back.

"Burke, the trouble with most ministers, and poets, and painters, and novelists, and law-makers, and other successful professional men who are supposed to show us common, working people the right way to go is that they don't get out and mix it up. They don't have to work for a mean boss, they don't know what it is to go hungry and starved and afraid to call your soul your own—scared by the salary envelope at the end of the week. They don't get out and make their *souls* sweat *blood*. Otherwise, they'd reform the world so quickly that men like Trubus wouldn't be able to make a living out of the charity game."

Barton smiled jovially.

"But here we go sermonizing. People don't want to listen to sermons all the time."

"Well, we're on a serious subject, and it means our bread and butter and our happiness in life, when you get right down to it," said Bobbie. "I don't like sermons myself. I'd rather live in the Garden of Eden, where they didn't need any. Wouldn't you?"

"Yes, but my wheel chair would find it rough riding without any clearings," said Barton. "By the way, Bob, I've some news for you. My lawyer is coming up here to-night, to talk over some patent matters, and you can lay your family matters before him. He'll attend to that and you may get justice done you. If you have some money back in Illinois, you ought to have it."

"He can get all he wants—if he gives me some," agreed Burke, "and I'll back your patents."

The old man started off again on his plans, and they argued and explained to each other as happy as two boys with some new toys, until the sisters came home.

Lorna was distinctly cool toward Burke, but, under a stern look from Mary, gave the outward semblance of good grace. The fact that he had been present in her home at the time of her disastrous escapade, even though she believed him ignorant of it, made the girl sensitive and aloof.

She left Mary alone with him at the earliest pretext, and Bobbie had interesting things to say to her: things which were nobody's business but theirs.

Barton's lawyer came before Burke left to report for evening duty, and he spent considerable effort to learn the story of the uncle and the curious will.

Now a digression in narrative is ofttimes a dangerous parting of ways. But on this particular day Bobbie Burke had come to a parting of the ways unwittingly. He had left the plodding life of routine excitement of the ordinary policeman to embark upon a journey fraught with multifold dangers. In addition to his enemies of the underworld, he had made a new one in an entirely different sphere.

To follow the line of digression, had the reader gone into the same building on Fifth Avenue which Burke had entered that afternoon, perhaps an hour later, and had he stopped on the third floor, entered a door marked "Mercantile Agency," he would have discovered a very busy little market-place. The first room of the suite of offices thus indicated was quite small. A weazened man, with thin shiny fingers, an unnaturally pallid face, and stooped shoulders, sat at a small flat-top desk, inside an iron grating of the kind frequently seen in cashiers' offices.

He watched the hall door with beady eyes, and whenever it opened to admit a newcomer he subjected that person to keen scrutiny; then he pushed a small button which automatically clicked a spring in the lock of the grated door.

This done, it was possible for the approved visitor to push past into a larger room shut off from the first office by a heavy door which invariably slammed, because it was pulled shut by a strong wire spring and was intended to slam.

The larger room opened out on a rear court, and, upon passing one of the large dirty windows, a fire escape could be descried. Around this room were a number of benches. Close scrutiny would have disclosed the fact that they were old-fashioned church pews, dismantled from some disused sanctuary. Two large tables were ranged in the center of the room.

The floor was extremely dirty. The few chairs were very badly worn, and the only decorations on the walls were pasted clippings of prize fighters and burlesque queens, cut from the pages of *The Police Gazette* and the sporting pages of some newspapers.

Into this room, all through the afternoon, streamed a curious medley of people. Tall men, small men, rough men, dapper men, and loudly dressed women, who for the most part seemed inclined to corpulence. They talked sometimes; many seemed well acquainted. Others appeared to be strangers, and they glanced about them uneasily, apparently suspicious of their fellows.

This seemed a curious waiting room for a Fifth Avenue "Mercantile Agency."

But inside the room to the left, marked "private," was the explanation of the mystery; at last there was a partial explanation of the curious throng.

As the occupants chatted, or kept frigid and uneasy silence, in the outer room a fat man, smooth of face and monkish in appearance, occasionally appeared at the private portal and admitted one person at a time.

After disappearing through this door, his visitors were not seen again, for they left by another door, which automatically closed and locked itself as they went directly into the hall corridor where the elevators ran.

In the private office of the "Mercantile Agency" the fat man would sit at his desk and listen attentively to the words of his visitor.

"Speak up, Joe. You know I'm hard of hearing—don't whisper to me," was the tenor of a remark which he seemed to direct to every visitor. Yet strangely enough he frequently stopped to listen to voices in the outer room, which he appeared to recognize without difficulty.

On this particular afternoon a dapper-dressed youth was an early caller.

"Well, Tom, what luck on the steamer? Now, don't swallow your voice. Remember, I got kicked in the ear by a horse before I quit bookmaking, and I have to humor my hearing."

"Oh, it was easy. That Swede, Jensen, came over, you know, and he had picked out a couple of peachy Swede girls who were going to meet their cousin at the Battery. Minnie and I went on board ship as soon as she docked, to meet our relatives, and we had a good look at 'em while they were lined up with the other steerage passengers. They were fine, and we got Jensen to take 'em up to the Bronx. They're up at Molloy's house overnight. It's better to keep 'em there, and give 'em some food. You know, the emigrant society is apt to be on the lookout to-day. The cousin was there when the ferry came in from the Island, all right, but we spotted him before the boat got in, and I had Mickey Brown pick a fight with him, just in time to get him pinched. He was four blocks away when the boat landed, and Jensen, who had made friends with the girls coming over, told them he would take 'em to his aunt's house until they heard from their cousin."

"What do they look like? We've got to have particulars, you know."

"Well, one girl is tall, and the other rather short. They both have yellow hair and cheeks like apples. One's name is Lena and the other Marda—the rest of their names was too much for me. They're both about eighteen years old, and well dressed, for Swedes."

The fat man was busy writing down certain data on a pad arranged in a curious metal box, which looked something like those on which grocers' clerks make out the order lists for customers.

"Say, Henry, what do you use that thing for? Why don't you use a fountain pen and a book?" asked the dapper one.

"That's my affair," snapped the fat man. "I want this for records, and I know how to do it. Go on. What did Mrs. Molloy pay you?"

"Well, you know she's a tight one. I had to argue with her, and I have a lot of expense on this, anyway."

"Go on—don't begin to beef about it. I know all about the expenses. We paid the preliminaries. Now, out with the money from Molloy. It was to be two hundred dollars, and you know it. Two hundred apiece is the exact figure."

The visitor stammered, and finally pulled out a roll of yellow-backed bills "Well, I haven't gotten mine yet," he whined.

"Yours is just fifty on this, for you've had a steamer assignment every day this week. You can give your friend Minnie a ten-spot. Now, report here to-morrow at ten, for I've a new line for you. Good day. Shut the door."

The fat man was accustomed to being obeyed. The other departed with a surly manner, as though he had received the worst of a bargain. The manager jotted down the figures on the revolving strip of paper, for such it was, while the pencil he used was connected by two little metal arms to the side of the mechanism. Some little wheels inside the register clicked, as he turned the paper lever over for a clean record. He put the money into his wallet.

He went to the door to admit another.

"Ah, Levy, what do you have to say?"

"Ah, Meester Clemm, eet's a bad bizness! Nattings at all to-day. I've been through five shoit-vaist factories, and not a girl could I get. Too much of dis union bizness. I told dem I vas a valking delegate, but I don't t'ink I look like a delegate. Vot's to be done?"

The manager looked at him sternly.

"Well, unless you get a wiggle on, you'll be back with a pushcart, where you belong, over on East Broadway, Levy. The factories are full of girls, and they don't make four dollars a week. Lots of pretty ones, and you know where we can place them. One hundred dollars apiece, if a girl is right, and that means twenty-five for you. You've been drawing money from me for three weeks without bringing in a cent. Now you get on the job. Try Waverley Place and come in here to-morrow. You're a good talker in Yiddish, and you ought to be able to get some action. Hustle out now. I can't waste time."

The manager jotted down another memorandum, and again his machine clicked, as he turned the lever.

A portly woman, adorned in willow plumes, sealskin cloak and wearing large rhinestones in her rings and necklace, now entered at the manager's signal.

"Well, Madame Blanche, what have you to report?"

"I swear I ain't had no luck, Mr. Clemm. Some one's put the gipsy curse on me. Twice this afternoon in the park I've seen two pretty girls, and each time I got chased by a cop. I got warned. I think they're gettin' wise up there around Forty-second Street and Sixth Avenue."

"Well, how about that order we had from New Orleans? That hasn't been paid yet. You know it was placed through you. You got your commish out of it, and this establishment always wants cash. No money orders, either. Spot cash. We don't monkey with the United States mail. There's too many city bulls looking around for us now to get Uncle Sam's men on the job."

The portly person under the willow plume, with a tearful face, began to wipe her eyes with a lace kerchief from which, emanated the odor of Jockey Club.

"Oh, Mr. Clemm, you are certainly the hardest man we ever had to do business with. I just can't pay now for that, with my high rents, and gettin' shook down in the precinct and all."

"Can it, Madame Blanche. I'm a business man. They're not doing any shaking down just now in your precinct. I know all about the police situation up there, for they've got a straight inspector. Now, I want that four hundred right now. We sent you just what was ordered and if I don't get the money right now you get blacklisted. Shell out!"

The manager's tone was hard as nails.

"Oh, Mr. Clemm ... well, excuse me. I must step behind your desk to get it, but you ain't treatin' me right, just the same, to force it this way."

Madame Blanche, with becoming modesty, stepped out of view in order to draw forth from their silken resting place four new one hundred dollar bills. She laid them gingerly and regretfully on the desk, where they were quickly snatched up by the business-like Clemm.

"Maybe I'll have a little order for next week, if you can give better terms, Mr. Clemm," began the lady, but the manager waved her aside.

"Nix, Madame. Get out. I'm busy. You know the terms, and I advise you not to try any more of this hold-out game. You're a week late now, and the next time you try it you'll be sorry. Hurry. I've got a lot of people to see."

She left, wiping her eyes.

The next man to enter was somewhat mutilated. His eye was blackened and the skin across his cheek was torn and just healing from a fresh cut.

"Well, well, well! What have you been up to, Barlow? A prize fight?" snapped Clemm.

"Aw, guv'nor, quit yer kiddin'. Did ye ever hear of me bein' in a fight? Nix. I tried to work dis needle gag over in Brooklyn an' I got run outen de t'eayter on me neck. Dere ain't no luck. I'd better go back to der dip ag'in."

"You stick to orders and stay around those cheap department stores, as you've been told to do, and you'll have no black eyes. Last month you brought in eleven hundred dollars for me, and you got three hundred of it yourself. What's the matter with you? You look like a panhandler? Don't you save your money? You've got to keep decently dressed."

"Aw, guv'nor, I guess it's easy come, easy go. Ain't dere nottin' special ye kin send me on?"

"Report here to-morrow at eleven. We're planning something pretty good. Here's ten dollars. Go rig yourself up a little better and get that eye painted out. Hustle up. I'm busy."

The dilapidated one took the bill and rolled his good eye in gratitude.

"Sure, guv'nor, you're white wid me. I kin always git treated right here."

"Don't thank me, it's business. Get out and look like a man when I see you next. I don't want any bums working for me."

The fat man jotted down a memorandum of his outlay on the little machine. Then he admitted the next caller.

"Ah, it's you, Jimmie. Well, what have you to say? You've been working pretty well, so Shepard tells me. What about his row the other night? I thought that girl was sure."

"Well, Mr. Clemm, ye see, we had it fixed all right, an' some foxy gink blows in wid a taxi an' lifts de dame right from outen Shepard's mit! De slickest getaway I ever seen. I don't know wot 'is game is, but he sure made some getaway, an' we never even got a smell at 'im."

"Who was with you on the deal? Who did the come-on?"

"Oh, pretty Baxter. You knows, w'en dat boy hands 'em de goo-goo an' wiggles a few Tangoes he's dere wid both feet! But dis girl was back on de job ag'in in her candy store next day. But Baxter'll git 'er yit. Shepard's pullin' dis t'eayter manager bull, so he'll git de game yet."

"Did her folks get wise?"

"Naw, not as we kin tell. Shepard he seen her once after she left de store. De trouble is 'er sister woiks in de same place. We got ter git dat girl fired, and den it'll be easy goin'. De goil gits home widout de sister findin' out about it, she tells Shepard. I don't quite pipe de dope on dis butt-in guy. But he sure spoiled Shepard's beauty fer a week. Dere's only one t'ing I kin suspect."

"All right, shoot it. You know I'm busy. This girl's worth the fight, for I know who wants one just about her looks and age. What is it? We'll work it if money will do it, for there's a lot of money in this or I wouldn't have all you fellows on the job. I saw a picture she gave Baxter. She's a pretty little chicken, isn't she?"

"Shoor! Some squab. Well, Mr. Clemm, dere's a rookie cop down in de precinct w'ere I got a couple workin', named Burke. Bobbie Burke, damn 'im! He gave me de worst beatin' up I ever got from any cop, an' I'm on bail now for General Sessions fer assaultin' 'im."

"What's he got to do with it?"

"Well, dis guy was laid up in de hospital by one of me pals who put 'im out on first wid a brick. He got stuck on a gal whose old man was in dat hospital, and dat gal is de sister of dis yere Lorna Barton. Does ye git me?"

Clemm's eyes sparkled.

"What does he look like? Brown hair, tall, very square shoulders?" he asked.

"Exact! He's a fresh guy wid his talk, too—one of dem ejjicated cops. Dey tells me he was a collige boy, or in de army or somethin'."

"Could he have known about Lorna Barton going out with Baxter that night Shepard was beaten?"

"My Gaud! Yes, cause Baxter he tells me Burke was dere at de house." Clemm nodded his head.

"Then you can take a hundred to one shot tip from me, Jimmie, that this Burke had something to do with Shepard. He may have put one of his friends on the job. Those cops are not such dummies as we think they are sometimes. That fellow's a dangerous man."

Clemm pondered for a moment. Jimmie was surprised, for the manager of the "Mercantile Agency" was noted for his rapid-fire methods. The Monk knew that something of great importance must be afoot to cause this delay.

The manager tapped the desk with his fingers, as he moved his lips, in a silent little conversation with himself. At last he banged the desk with vehemence.

"Here, Jimmie. I'm going to entrust you with an important job."

The Monk brightened and smiled hopefully.

"How much money would it take to put Officer Bobbie Burke, if that's his name, where the cats can't keep him awake at night?"

Jimmie looked shiftily at the manager.

"You mean..."

He drew his hand significantly across his throat, raising his heavy eyebrows in a peculiar monkey grimace which had won for him his soubriquet.

"Yes, to quiet his nerves. It's a shame to let these ambitious young policemen worry too much about their work."

"I kin git it done fer twenty-five dollars."

"Well, here's a hundred, for I'd like to have it attended to neatly, quietly and permanently. You understand me?"

"Say, I'm ashamed ter take money fer dis!" laughed Jimmie the Monk.

"Don't worry about that, my boy. Make a good job of it. It's just business. I'm buying the service and you're selling it. Now get out, for I've got a lot more marketing to do."

Jimmie got.

It was indeed a busy little market place, with many commodities for barter and trade.

CHAPTER X

WHEN THE TRAIN COMES IN

Burke was sent up to Grand Central Station the following morning by Captain Sawyer to assist one of the plain-clothes men in the apprehension of two well-known gangsters who had been reported by telegraph as being on their way to New York.

"We want them down in this precinct, Burke, and you have seen these fellows, so I want to have you keep a sharp lookout in the crowd when the train comes in. In case of a scuffle in a crowd, it's not bad to have a bluecoat ready, because the crowd is likely to take sides. Anyway, there's apt to be some of this gas-house gang up there to welcome them home. And your club will do more good than a revolver in a railroad station. You help out if Callahan gives you the sign, otherwise just monkey around. It won't take but a few minutes, anyway."

Burke went up to the station with the detective.

They watched patiently when the Chicago train came in, but there was no sign of the desired visitors. The detective entered the gate, when all the passengers had left, and searched the train.

"They must have gotten off at One Hundred and Twenty-fifth Street, from what the conductor could tell me. If they did, then they'll be nabbed up there, for Sawyer is a wise one, and had that planned," said Callahan. "I'll just loiter around the station a while to see any familiar faces. You can go back to your regular post, Burke."

Bobbie bade him good-bye, and started out one of the big entrances. As he did so he noticed a timid country girl, dressed ridiculously behind the fashions, and wearing an old-fashioned bonnet. She carried a rattan suitcase and two bandboxes.

"I wonder if she's lost," thought Burke. "I'll ask her. She looks scared enough."

He approached the young woman, but before he reached her a well-dressed young man accosted her. They exchanged a few words, and the fellow evidently gave her a direction, looking at a paper which she clutched in her nervous hand. The man walked quickly out of the building toward the street. Unseen by Burke, he whispered something to another nattily attired loiterer, an elderly man, who started toward the "car stop."

As Burke rounded the big pillar of the station entrance the man again addressed the country girl.

"There's your car, sis," he said, with a smile. Bobbie looked at him sharply.

There was something evil lurking in that smooth face, and the fellow stared impudently, with the haunting flicker of a scornful smile in his eyes, as he met the gaze of the policeman.

The country girl hurried toward the north-bound Madison Avenue car, which she boarded, with several other passengers. Among them was the gray-haired man who had received the mysterious message.

Burke watched the car disappear, and then turned to look at the smiling young man, who lit a cigarette, flicking the match insolently near the policeman's face.

"Move on, you," said Burke, and the young man shrugged his shoulders, leisurely returning to the waiting room of the station.

Burke was puzzled.

"I wonder what that game was? Maybe I stopped him in time. He looks like a cadet, I'll be bound. Well, I haven't time to stand around here and get a reprimand for starting on a wild-goose chase."

So Burke returned to the station house and started out on his rounds.

Had he taken the same car as the country girl, however, he would have understood the curious manoeuvre of the young man with the smile.

When the girl had ridden almost to the end of the line she left the car at a certain street. The elderly gentleman with the neat clothes and the fatherly gray hair did so at the same time. She walked uncertainly down one street, while he followed, without appearing to do so, on the opposite side. He saw her looking at the slip of paper, while she struggled with her bandboxes. He casually crossed over to the same side of the thoroughfare.

"Can I direct you, young lady?" he politely asked.

He was such a kind-looking old gentleman that the girl's confidence was easily won.

"Yes, sir. I'm looking for the Young Women's Christian Association. I thought it was down town, but a gentleman in the depot said it was on that street where I got off. I don't see it at all. They're all private houses, around here. You know, I've never been in New York City before, and I'm kinder green."

"Well, well, I wouldn't have known it," said her benefactor. "The Y.W.C.A. is down this street, just in the next block. You'll see the sign on the door, in big white letters. I've often passed it on my way to church."

"Oh, thank you, sir," and the country girl started on her quest once more, with a firmer grip on the suitcase and the bandboxes.

Sure enough, on the next block was a brownstone building—more or less dilapidated in appearance, it is true—just as he had prophesied.

There were the big white letters painted on a sign by the door. The girl went up the steps, rang the bell, and was admitted by a tousled, smirking negress.

"Is this here the Y.W.C.A.?" she asked nervously.

"Yassim!" replied the darkie. "Come right in, ma'am, and rest yoh bundles."

The girl stepped inside the door, which closed with a click that almost startled her. She backed to the door and put her hand on the knob. It did not turn!

"Are you *sure* this is the Y.W.C.A.?" she insisted. "I thought it was a great big building."

"Oh, yas, lady; dis is it. Yoh all don't know how nice dis buildin' is ontel you go through it. Gimme yoh things."

The negress snatched the suitcase from the girl's hand and whisked one of the bandboxes from the other.

"Here, you let go of that grip. I got all my clothes in there, and I don't think I'm in the right place."

As she spoke a plump lady, wearing rhinestone rings and a necklace of the same precious tokens, whom the reader might have recognized as no other than the tearful Madame Blanche, stepped from the parlor.

"Oh, my dear little girl. I'm so glad you came. We were expecting you. I am the president of the Y.W.C.A., you know. Just go right upstairs with Sallie, she'll show you to your room."

"Expecting me? How could you be? I didn't send word I was coming. I just got the address from our minister, and I lost part of it."

"That's all right, dearie. Just follow Sallie; you see she is taking your clothes up to your room. I'll be right up there, and see that you are all comfortable."

The bewildered girl followed the only instinct which asserted itself—that was to follow all her earthly belongings and get possession of them again. She walked into the trap and sprang up the stairs, two steps at a time, to overtake the negress.

Madame Blanche watched her lithe grace and strength as she sped upwards with the approving eye of a connoisseur.

"Fine! She's a beauty—healthy as they make 'em, and her cheeks are redder than mine, and mine cost money—by the box. Oh, here comes Pop."

She turned as the door was opened from the outside. It was a door which required the key from the inside, on certain occasions, and it was still arranged for the easy ingress of a visitor.

"Well, Blanche, what do you think?" inquired the benevolent old gentleman who had been such an opportune guide to the girl from up-State.

"Pop, she's a dandy. Percy can certainly pick 'em on the fly, can't he?"

"Well, don't I deserve a little credit?" asked the old gentleman, his vanity touched.

"Yes, you're our best little Seeing-Noo-Yorker. But say, Pop, Percy just telephoned me in time. We had to paint out that old sign, "help wanted," and put on 'Y.W.C.A.' Sallie is a great sign painter. We'll have trouble with this girl. She's a husky. But won't Clemm roll his eyes when he sees her?"

"Naw, he don't regard any of 'em more than a butcher does a new piece of beef. He's a regular business man, that's all. No pride in his art, nor nothing like that," sighed Pop. "But that girl made a hit with me, old as I am. She's a peach."

"Well, she won't look so rosy when Shepard shows her that she's got to mind. He's a rough one, he is. It gets on my nerves sometimes. They yell so, and he's got this whip stuff down too strong. You know I think he's act'ally crazy about beatin' them girls, and makin' them agree to go wherever we send 'em. He takes too much fun out of it, and when he welts 'em up it lowers the value. He'll be up this afternoon. We must have him ease it up a bit."

"Oh, well, he's young, ye know," said Pop. "Boys will be boys, and some of 'em's rough once in a while. I was a boy myself once." And he pulled his white mustache vigorously as he smiled at himself in the large hall mirror.

"You'd better be off down to the station again, Pop," said Madame Blanche. "They're going to send over two Swedish girls from Molloy's in the Bronx this afternoon, and then put 'em on through to St. Paul. I've got a friend out there who wants 'em to visit her. Then Baxter telephoned me that he had a little surprise for me, later to-day. He's been quiet lately, and it's about time, or he'll have to get a job in the chorus again to pay his manicure bills."

Pop took his departure, and, as Sallie came down the stairs with a smile of duty done, Madame Blanche could hear muffled screams from above.

"Where is she, Sallie?"

"She's in de receibin' room, Madame. Jes' let 'er yowl. It'll do her good. I done' tol' er to save her breaf, but she is extravagant. Wait ontil Marse Shepard swings dat whip. She'll have sompen to sing about!"

And Sallie went about her duties—to put out the empty beer bottles for the brewery man and to give the prize Pomeranian poodle his morning bath.

Madame Blanche retired to her cosy parlor, where, beneath the staring eyes of her late husband's crayon portrait, and amused by the squawking of her parrot, she could forget the cares of her profession in the latest popular problem novel.

On the floor above a miserable, weeping country lassie was beating her hands against the thick door of the windowless dark room until they were bruised and bleeding.

She sank to her knees, praying for help, as she had been taught to do in her simple life back in the country town.

But her prayers seemed to avail her naught, and she finally sank, swooning, with her head against the cruel barrier. Back in the railroad station, Percy and his kind-faced assistant, Pop, were prospecting for another recruit.

CHAPTER XI

THE POISONED NEEDLE

That afternoon Burke improved his time, during a two-hour respite, to hunt for a birthday present for Mary.

Manlike, he was shy of shops, so he sought one of the big department stores on Sixth Avenue, where he instinctively felt that everything under the sun could be bought.

As Bobbie paused before one of the big display windows on the sidewalk he caught a glimpse of a familiar figure. It was that instinct which one only half realizes in a brief instant, yet which leaves a strong reaction of memory.

"Who was that?" he thought, and then remembered: Baxter.

Burke followed the figure which had passed him so quickly, and found the same dapper young man deeply engrossed in the window display of women's walking suits.

"What can he find so interesting in that window?" mused Burke. "I'll just watch his tactics. I don't believe that fellow is ever any place for any good!"

He stood far out on the sidewalk, close to the curb. The passing throng swept in two eddying, opposite currents between him and Baxter, whose attention seemed strictly upon the window.

"Well, there's his refined companion," was Burke's next impression, as he espied the effeminate figure of Craig, strolling along the sidewalk close to the same window.

"Can they be pickpockets? I would guess that was too risky for them to take a chance on."

Neither youth spoke to the other, although they walked very close to each other. As Burke scrutinized their actions he saw a young girl, tastefully dressed in a black velvet suit, with a black hat, turn about excitedly. She looked about her, as though in alarm, and her face was distorted with pain. Baxter gave her a shifty look and followed her. Craig had been close at her side.

Burke drew nearer to the girl. She seemed to falter, as she walked, and it was apparently with great effort that she neared the door of the big department store. Baxter was watching her stealthily now.

"Oh!" she exclaimed desperately and keeled backward. Baxter's calculations were close, for he caught her in his arms.

"Quick! Quick!" he cried to the big uniformed carriage attendant at the door. "Get me a taxicab. My sister has fainted."

The man whistled for a machine, as Burke watched them. The officer was calculating his own chances on what baseball players call a "double play." Craig was close behind Baxter, in the curious crowd. Burke guessed that it would take at least a minute or two for Baxter to get the girl into a machine. So he rushed for Craig and surprised that young gentleman with a vicious grasp of the throat.

"Help! Police!" cried Craig, as some women screamed. His wish was doubly answered, for Burke's police whistle was in his mouth and he blew it shrilly. A traffic squad man rushed across from the middle of the street.

"Hurry, I want to get my sister away!" ordered Baxter excitedly to the door man. "You big boob, what's the matter with you?"

The crowd of people about him shut off the view of Burke's activities fifteen feet away. Baxter was nervous and was doing his best to make a quick exit with his victim.

"What's this?" gruffly exclaimed the big traffic policeman, as he caught Craig's arm.

"The needle!" grunted Burke. "Here, I've got it from his pocket."

He drew forth a small hypodermic needle syringe from Craig's coat pocket, and held it up.

"It's a frame-up!" squealed Craig.

"Take him quick. I want to save the girl!" exclaimed Burke, as he rushed toward Baxter.

That young man was just pushing the girl into the taxicab when a middle-aged woman rushed out from the store entrance.

"That's my daughter Helen! Helen, my child!"

At this there was terrific confusion in the crowd, and Burke saw Baxter give the girl a rough shove away from the taxicab door. He slipped a bill into the chauffeur's willing hand and muttered an order. The car sprang forward on the instant.

"I'll get that fellow this time!" muttered Burke. "He hasn't seen me, and I'll trail him."

He turned about and espied a big gray racing car drawn up at the curb. A young man weighted down under a heavy load of goggles, fur and other racing appurtenances sat in the car. Its engines were humming merrily.

"Say, you, follow that car for me," sung out Officer 4434, delighted at his discovery. "The taxicab with the black body."

The driver of the racer snorted contemptuously.

"Do you know who *I* am?"

Burke wasted no time, but jumped into the seat, for it was as opportune as though placed there by Providence. Perhaps Providence has more to do with some coincidences than the worldly wise are prone to confess.

"*I'm* Officer 4434 of the Police Department, and you mind my orders."

"Well, I'm Reggie Van Nostrand," answered the young man, "and I take orders from no man."

Burke knew this young millionaire by reputation. But he was nowise daunted. He kept his eye on the distant taxicab, which had luckily been halted at the second cross street by the delayed traffic.

"I'm going to put this pretty car of yours in the scrap heap, and I'm going to land you in jail, with all your money," calmly replied Burke, drawing his revolver. "The man in that taxi is a white slaver who just tried the poison needle on a girl, and you and I are going to capture him."

The undeniable sporting blood surged in the veins of Reggie Van Nostrand, be it said to his credit. It was not the threat.

"I'm with you, Officer!" He pressed a little lever with his foot and the big racing machine sprang forward like a thing possessed by a demon of speed.

The traffic officer on the other street tried to stop the car, until he saw the uniform of the policeman in the seat.

Bob waved his hand, and the fixed post man held back several machines, in order to give him the right of way.

They were now within a block of the other car.

"Say, haven't you another robe or coat that I can put on to cover my uniform, for that fellow will suspect a chase, anyway?"

"Yes, there at your feet," replied Van Nostrand shortly. "It's my father's. He'll be wondering who stole me and the car. Let him wonder."

Burke pulled up the big fur coat and drew it around his shoulders as the car rumbled forward. He found a pair of goggles in a pocket of the coat.

"I don't need a hat with these to mask me," he exclaimed. "Now, watch out on your side of the car, and I'll do it on mine, for he's a sly one, and will turn down a side street."

They did well to keep a lookout, for suddenly the pursued taxi turned sharply to the right.

After it they went—not too close, but near enough to keep track of its manoeuvres.

"He's going up town now!" said Reggie Van Nostrand, when the car had diverged from the congested district to an open avenue which ran north and south. The machine turned and sped along merrily toward Harlem.

"We're willing," said Burke. "I want to track him to his headquarters."

Block after block they followed the taxicab. Sometimes they nosed along, at Burke's suggestion, so far behind that it seemed as though a quick turn to a side street would lose their quarry. But it was evident that Baxter had a definite destination which he wished to reach in a hurry.

At last they saw the car stop, and then the youth ahead dismounted.

He was paying the chauffeur as they whizzed past, apparently giving him no heed.

But before they had gone another block Burke deemed it safe to stop.

He signaled Van Nostrand, who shut off the power of the miraculous car almost as easily as he had started it. Burke nearly shot over the windshield with the momentum.

"Some car!" he grunted. "You make it behave better than a horse, and I think it has more brains."

Nothing in the world could have pleased the millionaire more than this. He was an eager hunter himself by now.

"Say, supposing I take off my auto coat and run down that street and see where he goes to?"

"Good idea. I'll wait for you in the machine, if you're not afraid of the police department."

"You bet I'm not. Here, I'll put on this felt hat under the seat. They won't suspect me of being a detective, will they?"

"Hardly," laughed Burke, as the young society man emerged from his chrysalis of furs and goggles, immaculately dressed in a frock coat. He drew out an English soft hat and even a cane. "You are ready for war or peace, aren't you?"

Van Nostrand hurried down the street and turned the corner, changing his pace to one of an easy and debonair grace befitting the possessor of several racing stables of horses and machines.

He saw his man a few hundred yards down the street. Van Nostrand watched him sharply, and saw him hesitate, look about, and then turn to the left. He ascended the steps of a dwelling.

By the time Van Nostrand had reached the house, to pass it with the barest sidelong glance, the pursued had entered and closed the door. The millionaire saw, to his surprise, a white sign over the door, "Swedish Employment Bureau." The words were duplicated in Swedish.

"That's a bally queer sign!" muttered Reggie. "And a still queerer place for a crook to go. I'll double around the block."

As he turned the corner he saw an old-fashioned cab stop in front of the house. Two men assisted a woman to alight, unsteadily, and helped her up the steps.

"Well, she must be starving to death, and in need of employment," commented the rich young man. "I think the policeman has brought me to a queer hole. I'll go tell him about it."

The fashionable set who dwell on the east side of Central Park would have spilled their tea and cocktails about this time had they seen the elegant Reggie Van Nostrand breaking all speed records as he dashed down the next street, with his cane in one hand and his hat in the other. He reached the car, breathless, but his tango athletics had stood him in good stead.

"What's up?" asked Burke, jumping from the seat.

"Why, that's a Swedish employment agency, and I saw two men lead a woman up the steps from a cab just now. What shall we do?"

"You run your machine to the nearest drug store and find out where the nearest police station is. Then get a few cops in your machine, and come to that house, for you'll find me there," ordered Burke. "How far down the block?"

"Nearly to the next corner," answered Reggie, who leaped into his racing seat and started away like the wind.

Burke hurried down, following the path of the other, until he came to the house. He looked at the sign, and then glanced about him. He saw an automobile approaching, and intuitively stepped around the steps of the house next door, into the basement entry.

He had hardly concealed himself when the machine stopped in front of the other dwelling.

A big Swede, still carrying his emigrant bundle, descended from the machine, and called out cheerily in his native language to the occupants within the vehicle. Burke, peeping cautiously, saw two buxom Swedish lassies, still in their national costumes, step down to the street. The machine turned and passed on down the street.

Burke saw the man point out the sign of the employment agency, and the girls chattered gaily, cheered up with hopes of work, as he led them up the steps.

The door closed behind them.

Burke quietly walked around the front of the house and up the steps after them. He had made no noise as he ascended, and as he stood by the wall of the vestibule he fancied he detected a bitter cry, muffled to an extent by the heavy walls.

He examined the sign, and saw that it was suspended by a small wire loop from a nail in the door jamb.

Bobbie reached upward, took the sign off its hook, and turned it about.

"Well, just as I thought!" he exclaimed.

On the reverse side were the tell-tale letters, "Y.W.C.A."

"They are ready for all kinds of customers. I wonder how they'll like me!" was the humorous thought which flitted through his mind as he quietly turned the knob. It opened readily.

Bobbie stood inside the hallway, face to face with the redoubtable Pop!

Pop's eyes protruded as they beheld this horrid vision of a bluecoat. A cynical smile played about Burke's pursed lips as he held the sign up toward the old reprobate.

"Can I get a job here? Is there any work for me to do in this employment agency?" he drawled quietly.

Pop acted upon the instinct which was the result of many years' dealings with minions of the law. He had been a contributor to the "cause" back in the days of Boss Tweed. He temporarily forgot that times had changed.

"That's all right, pal," he said, with a sickly smile, "just a little token for the wife and kids."

He handed out a roll of bills which he pressed against Bobbie's hands. The policeman looked at him with a curious squint.

"So, you think that will fix me, do you?"

"Well, if you're a little hard up, old fellow, you know I'm a good fellow...."

Up the stairs there was a scuffle.

Bobbie heard another scream. So, before Pop could utter another sound he pushed the old man aside and rushed up, three steps at a time. The first door he saw was locked—behind it Bobbie knew a woman was being mistreated.

He rushed the door and gave it a kick with his stout service boots.

A chair was standing in the hall. He snatched this up and began smashing at the door, directing vigorous blows at the lock. The first leg broke off. Then the second. The third was smashed, but the fourth one did the trick. The door swung open, and as it did so a water pitcher, thrown with precision and skill, grazed his forehead. Only a quick dodge saved him from another skull wound.

Burke sprang into the room.

There were three men in it, while Madame Blanche, the proprietress of the miserable establishment, stood in the middle transfixed with fear. She still held in her hand the black snake whip with which she had been "taming" one of the sobbing Swedish girls. The Swede held one of his country-women in a rough grip.

The country girl, who had been hitherto locked in the closet, was down on her knees, her bruised hands outstretched toward Burke.

"Oh, save me!" she cried.

The last of the victims, who was evidently unconscious from a drug, was lying on the floor in a pathetic little heap.

Baxter was cowering behind the bed.

The barred windows, placed there to prevent the escape of the unfortunate girl prisoners, were their Nemesis, for they were at the mercy of the lone policeman.

"Drop that gun!" snapped Burke, as he saw the Swede reaching stealthily toward a pocket.

His own, a blue-steeled weapon, was swinging from side to side as he covered them.

"Hands up, every one, and march down these stairs before me!" he ordered. Just then he heard a footstep behind him. Old Pop was creeping up the steps with Madame Blanche's carving knife, snatched hastily from the dining-room table.

Burke, cat-like, caught a side glance of this assailant, and he swung completely around, kicking Pop below the chin. That worthy tumbled down the stairs with a howl of pain.

"Now, I'm going to shoot to kill. Every court in the state will sustain a policeman who shoots a white-slaver. Don't forget that!" cried Burke sharply. "You girls let them go first."

"I'm going to shoot to kill. Every court in the state will sustain a policeman who shoots a white-slaver."

Down the steps went the motley crew, backing slowly at Burke's order. The girls, sobbing hysterically with joy at their rescue, almost impeded the bluecoat's defense as they clung to his arms.

It was a curious procession which met the eyes of Reggie Van Nostrand and half a dozen reserves who had just run up the steps.

"Well, I say old chap, isn't this jolly?" cried Reggie. "This beats any show I ever saw! Why, it's a regular Broadway play!"

"You bet it is, and you helped me well. The papers ought to give you a good spread to-morrow, Mr. Van Nostrand," answered Bobbie grimly, as he shook the young millionaire's hand with warmth. The gang were rapidly being handcuffed by the reserves.

Bobbie turned toward Baxter. It was a great moment of triumph for him. "Well, Baxter, so I got you at last! You're the pretty boy who takes young girls out to turkey trots! Now, you can join a dancing class up the Hudson, and learn the new lock-step glide!"

CHAPTER XII

THE REVENGE OF JIMMIE THE MONK

At the uptown station house Burke and his fellow officers had more than a few difficulties to surmount. The two Swedish girls were hysterical with fright, and stolid as the people of northern Europe generally are, under the stress of their experience the young women were almost uncontrollable. It was not until some gentle matrons from the Swedish Emigrant Society had come to comfort them in the familiar tongue that they became normal enough to tell their names and the address of the unfortunate cousin. This man was eventually located and he led his kinswomen off happy and hopeful once more.

Sallie, the negress, was remanded for trial, in company with her sobbing mistress, who realized that she was facing the certainty of a term of years in the Federal prison.

Uncle Sam and his legal assistants are not kind to "captains of industry" in this particular branch of interstate commerce.

"We have the goods on them," said the Federal detective who had been summoned at once to go over the evidence to be found in the carefully guarded house of Madame Blanche. "This place, to judge from the records has been run along two lines. For one thing, it is what we term a 'house of call.' Madame Blanche has a regular card index of at least two hundred girls."

"Then, that gives a pretty good list for you to get after, doesn't it?" said Burke, who was joining in the conference between the detective, the captain of the precinct, and the inspector of the police district.

"Well, the list won't do much good. About all you can actually prove is that these girls are bad ones. There's a description of each girl, her age, her height, her complexion and the color of her hair. It's horribly business like," replied the detective. "But I'm used to this. We don't often get such a complete one for our records. This list alone is no proof against the girls—even if it does give the list price of their shame, like the tag on a department store article. This woman has been keeping what you might call an employment agency by telephone. When a certain type of girl is wanted, with a certain price—and that's the mark of her swellness, as you might call it—Madame Blanche is called up. The girl is sent to the address given, and she, too, is given her orders over the telephone; so you see nothing goes on in this house which would make it strictly within the law as a house of ill repute."

"But, do you think there is much of this particular kind of trade?" queried Bobbie. "I've heard a lot of this sort of thing. But I put down a great deal of it to the talk of men who haven't anything else much to discuss."

"There certainly is a lot of it. When the police cleaned up the old districts along Twenty-ninth Street and Thirtieth and threw the regular houses out of the business, the call system grew up. These girls, many of them, live in quiet boarding houses and hotels where they keep up a strict appearance of decency—and yet they are living the worst kind of immoral lives, because they follow this trade scientifically."

Reggie Van Nostrand, by reason of his gallant assistance, and at his urgent request, had been allowed to listen.

"By George, gentlemen, I have a lot of money that I don't know what to do with. I wish there was some way I could help in getting this sort of thing stopped. Here's my life—I've been a silly spender of a lot of money my great grandfather made because he bought a farm and never sold it—right in the heart of what is now the busy section of town. I can't think of anything very bad that I've done, and still less any good that will amount to anything after I die. I'm going to spend some of what I don't need toward helping the work of cleaning out this evil."

The inspector grunted.

"Well, young man, if you spend it toward letting people know just how bad conditions are, and not covering the truth up or not trying to reform humanity by concealing the ugly things, you may do a lot. But don't be a *reformer.*"

"What can be done with this woman Blanche?" asked Van Nostrand meekly.

"She'll be put where she won't have to worry about telephone calls and card indexes. Every one of these girls should be locked up, and given a good strong hint to get a job. It won't do much good. But, we've got this much of their records, and will be able to drive some of them out of the trade. When every big city keeps on driving them out, and the smaller cities do the same, they'll find that it's easier to give up silk dresses forever and get other work than to starve to death. But you can't get every city in the country doing this until the men and women of influence, the mothers and fathers are so worked up over the rottenness of it all that they want to house-clean their own surroundings."

"One thing that should be done in New York and other towns is to put the name of the owner of every building on a little tablet by the door. If that was done here in New York," said the inspector, "you'd be surprised to see how much real estate would be sold by church vestries, charitable organizations, bankers, old families, and other people who get big profits from the high rent that a questionable tenant is willing to pay."

"Madame Blanche, and these poor specimens of manhood with her are guilty of trafficking in girls for sale in different states. These Swedes were to be sent to Minnesota, and her records show that she has been supplying the Crib, in New Orleans, and what's left of the Barbary Coast in Chicago. Why, she has sent six girls to the Beverly Club in Chicago during the last month."

"Where does she get them all?" asked Burke. "I've been trailing some of these gangsters, but they certainly can't supply them all, like this."

The detective shook his head, and spoke slowly.

"There are about three big clearing houses of vice in New York, and they are run by men of genius, wealth and enormous power. I'm going to run them down yet. You've helped on this, Officer Burke. If you can do more and get at the men higher up—there's not a mention of their location in all of Blanche's accounts, not a single check book—then, you will get a big reward from the Department of Justice. For Uncle Sam is not sleeping with the enemy inside his fortifications."

Burke's eyes snapped with the fighting spirit.

"I've been doing my best with them since I got on the force, and I hope to do more if they don't finish me first. A little Italian fruit man down in my precinct sent word to me to-day that they were 'after me.' So, maybe I will not have a chance."

Van Nostrand interrupted at this point.

"Well, Officer 4434, you can have the backing of all the money you need as far as I am concerned. You'll have to come down to my offices some day soon, and we'll work out a plan of getting after these people. Can I do anything more, inspector?"

The official shook his head.

"There's a poor young woman here who is half drugged, and doesn't know who she is," he began.

"Well, send her to some good private hospital and have her taken care of and send the bill to me," said Reggie. "I've got to be getting downtown. Goodbye, Officer Burke, don't forget me."

"Goodbye—you've been a fine chauffeur and a better detective," said the young policeman, "even if you are a millionaire." And the two young men laughed with an unusual cordiality as they shook hands. Despite the difference in their stations it was the similarity of red blood in them both which melted away the barriers, and later developed an unconventional and permanent friendship between them.

Burke talked with Henrietta Bailey, the country girl, who sat dejectedly in the station house. She had no plans for the future, having come to the big city to look for a position, trusting in the help of the famous Y.W.C.A. organization, of whose good deeds and protection she had heard so much, even in the little town up state.

"I'll call them up, down at their main offices," said Bobbie, "but it's a big society and they have all they can do. Wouldn't you like to meet a nice sweet girl who will take a personal interest in you, and go down there with you herself?"

Henrietta tried to hold back the tears.

"Oh, land sakes," she began, stammering, "I ... do ... want to just blubber on somebody's shoulder. I'm skeered of all these New York folks, and I'm so lonesome, Mr. Constable."

"We'll just cure that, then," answered Burke. "I'll introduce you to the very finest girl in the world, and she'll show you that hearts beat as warmly in a big city as they do in a village of two hundred people."

Bobbie lost no time in telephoning Mary Barton, who was just on the point of leaving Monnarde's candy store.

She came directly uptown to meet the country girl and take her to the modest apartment for the night.

Bobbie devoted the interim to making his report on the unusual circumstances of his one-man raid ... and dodging the police reporters who were on the scene like hawks as soon as the news had leaked out.

Despite his declaration that the credit should go to the precinct in which the arrests had been made half a dozen photographers, with their black artillery-like cameras had snapped views of the house, and some grotesque portraits of the young officer. Other camera men, with newspaper celerity, had captured the aristocratic features of Reggie Van Nostrand and his racing car, as he sat in it before his Fifth Avenue club. It was such a story that city editors gloated over, and it was to give the embarrassed policeman more trouble than it was worth.

Bobbie's telephone report to Captain Sawyer, explaining his absence from the downtown station house was greeted with commendation.

"That's all right, Burke, go as far as you like. A few more cases like that and you'll be on the honor list for the Police Parade Day. Clean it up as soon as you can," retorted his superior.

When Mary took charge of Henrietta Bailey, the hapless girl felt as though life were again worth living. After a good cry in the matron's room, she was bundled up, her rattan suitcase and the weather-beaten band boxes were carried over to the Barton home.

"I don't know whether you had better say anything about this Baxter to Lorna or not," said Bobbie, as he stood outside the house, to start on his way downtown. "It's a horrible affair, and her escape from the man's clutches was a close one."

"She's cured now, however," stoutly declared Mary. "I have no fears for Lorna."

"Then do as you think best. I'll see you to-morrow afternoon, there at the store, and you can take supper downtown with me if you would like. If there is any way I can help about this girl let me know."

They separated, and Mary took her guest upstairs.

Her father was greatly excited for he had just put the finishing touches on his dictagraph-recorder. His mind was so over-wrought with his work that Mary thought it better not to tell him of the exciting afternoon until later. She simply introduced Henrietta as a friend from the country who was going to spend the night. Lorna was courteous enough to the newcomer, but seemed abstracted and dreamy. She neglected the little household duties, making the burden harder for Mary. Henrietta's rustic training, however, asserted itself, and she gladly took a hand in the preparation of the evening meal.

"I've a novel I want to finish reading, Mary," said her sister, "and if you don't mind I'm going to do it. You and Miss Bailey don't need me. I'll go into our room until supper is ready."

"What is it, dear? It must be very interesting," replied Mary, a shade of uneasiness coming over her. "You are not usually so literary after the hard work at the store all day."

Lorna laughed.

"It's time I improved my mind, then. A friend gave it to me—it's the story of a chorus girl who married a rich club man, by Robin Chalmers, and oh, Mary! It's simply the most exciting thing you ever read. The stage does give a girl chances that she never gets working in a store, doesn't it?"

"There are several kinds of chances, Lorna," answered the older girl slowly. "There are many girls who beautify their own lives by their success on the stage, but you know, there are a great many more who find in that life a terrible current to fight against. While they may make large salaries, as measured against what you and I earn, they must rehearse sometimes for months without salary at all. If the show is successful they are in luck for a while, and their pictures are in every paper. They spend their salary money to buy prettier clothes and to live in beautiful surroundings, and they gauge their expenditures upon what they are earning from week to week. But girls I have known tell me that is the great trouble. For when the play loses its popularity, or fails, they have accustomed themselves to extravagant tastes, and they must rehearse for another show, without money coming in."

"Oh, but a clever girl can pick out a good opportunity."

"No, she can't. She is dependent upon the judgment of the managers, and if you watch and see that two of every three shows put on right in New York never last a month out, you'll see that the managers' judgment is not so very keen. Even the best season of a play hardly lasts thirty weeks—a little over half a year, and so you must divide a girl's salary in two to find what she makes in a year's time. You and I, in the candy store, are making more money than a girl who gets three times the money a week on the stage, for we have a whole year of work, and we don't have to go to manicures and modistes and hairdressers two or three times a week."

"Well, I wish we did!" retorted Lorna petulantly. "There's no romance in you, Mary. You're just humdrum and old-fashioned and narrow. Think of the beautiful costumes, and the lights, the music, the applause of thousands! Oh, it must be wonderful to thrill an audience, and have hundreds of men worshiping you, and all that, Mary."

Her sister's eyes filled with tears as she turned away.

"Go on with your book, Lorna," she murmured. "Maybe some day you'll read one which will teach you that old fashions are not so bad, that there's romance in home and that the true, decent love of one man is a million times better than the applause, and the flowers, and the flattery of hundreds. I've read such books."

"Hum!" sniffed Lorna, "I don't doubt it. Written by old maids who could never attract a man, nor look pretty themselves. Well, none of the girls I know bother with such books: there are too many lively ones written nowadays. Call me when supper is ready, for I'm hungry."

And she adjusted her curls before flouncing into the bedroom to lose herself in the adventures of the patchouli heroine.

It was a quiet evening at the Barton home. The father was too engrossed to give more than abstracted heed, even to the appetizing meal. Mary forbore to interrupt his thoughts about the new machine. She felt a hesitation about narrating the afternoon's adventures of Bobbie Burke to Lorna, for the girl seemed estranged and eager only for the false romance of her novel. With Henrietta, Mary discussed the opportunities for work in the great city, already overcrowded with struggling girls. So convincing was she, the country lass decided that she would take the train next morning back to the little town where she could be safe from the excitement and the dangers of the city lure.

"I reckon I'm a scared country mouse," she declared. "But I'm old enough to know a warning when I get one. The Lord didn't intend me to be a city girl, or he wouldn't have given me this lesson to-day. I've got my old grand dad up home, and there's Joe Mills, who is foreman in the furniture factory. I think I'd better get back and help Joe spend his eighteen a week in the little Clemmons house the way he wanted me to do."

"You couldn't do a better thing in the world," said Mary, patting her hand gently as they sat in the cosy little kitchen. "Your little town would be a finer place to bring up little Joes and little Henriettas than this big city, wouldn't it? And I don't believe the right Joe ever comes but once in a girl's life. There aren't many fellows who are willing to share eighteen a week with a girl in New York."

Mary's guest blushed happily as the light of a new determination shone in her eyes. She opened a locket which she wore on a chain around her neck.

"I always thought Joe was nice, and all that—but I read these here stories about the city fellers, and I seen the pictures in the magazines, and thought Joe was a rube. But he ain't, is he?"

She held up the little picture, as she opened the locket, for Mary's scrutiny. The honest, smiling face, the square jaw, the clear eyes of Joe looked forth as though in greeting of an old friend.

"You can't get back to Joe any too quickly," advised Mary, and Henrietta wiped her eyes. She had received a homeopathic cure of the city madness in one brief treatment!

It was not a quiet evening for Officer 4434.

When he emerged from the Subway at Fourteenth Street a newsboy approached him with a bundle of papers.

"Uxtry! Uxtry!" shouted the youngster. "Read all about de cop and de millionaire dat captured de white slavers!"

The lad shoved a paper at Bobbie, who tossed him a nickel and hurried on, quizzically glancing at the flaring headlines which featured the name of Reggie Van Nostrand and his own. The quickly made illustrations, showing his picture, the machine of the young clubman, and the house of slavery were startling. The traditional arrow indicated "where the battle was fought," and Burke laughed as he studied the sensational report.

"Well, I look more like a gangster, according to this picture, than Jimmie the Monk! Those news photographers don't flatter a fellow very much."

At the station house he was warmly greeted by his brother officers. It was embarrassing, to put it mildly; Burke had no desire for a pedestal.

"Oh, quit it, boys," he protested. "You fellows do more than this every day of your lives. I'm only a rookie and I know it. I don't want this sort of thing and wish those fool reporters had minded their own business."

"That's all right, Bobbie," said Doctor MacFarland, who had dropped in on his routine call, "you'd better mind your own p's and q's, for you will be a marked man in this neighborhood. It's none too savory at best. You know how these gunmen hate any policeman, and now they've got your photograph and your number they won't lose a minute to use that knowledge. Keep your eyes on all points of the compass when you go out to-night."

"I'll try not to go napping, Doc," answered Burke gratefully. "You're a good friend of mine, and I appreciate your advice. But I don't expect any more trouble than usual."

After his patrol duty Burke was scheduled for a period on fixed post. It was the same location as that on which he had made the acquaintance of Jimmie the Monk and Dutch Annie several months before. As a coincidence, it began to storm, just as it had on that memorable evening, except that instead of the blighting snow blizzards, furious sheets of rain swept the dirty streets, and sent pedestrians under the dripping shelter of vestibules and awnings.

Burke, without the protection of a raincoat, walked back and forth in the small compass of space allowed the peg-post watcher, beating his arms together to warm himself against the sickening chill of his dripping clothes.

As he waited he saw a man come out of the corner saloon.

It was no other than Shultberger, the proprietor of the café and its cabaret annex. The man wore a raincoat, and a hat pulled down over his eyes. He came to the middle of the crossing and closely scrutinized the young policeman.

"Is dot you, Burke?" he asked gruffly.

"Yes, what do you want of me?"

"Veil, I joost vanted to know dat a good man vos on post to-night, for I expect troubles mit dese gun-men. Dey don't like me, und I t'ought I'd find out who vos here."

This struck 4434 as curious. He knew that Shultberger was the guardian angel of the neighborhood toughs in time of storm and trouble. Yet he was anxious to do his duty.

"What's the trouble? Are they starting anything?"

The saloon man shook his head as he started back to his café.

"Oh, no. But ve all know vot a fighter you vos to-day. De papers is full mit it. Dey've got purty picture of you, too. I joost vos skeered dot dey might pick on me because I vos always running a orderly place, und because I'm de frend of de police. I'll call you if I need you."

He disappeared in the doorway.

Burke watched him, thinking hard. Perhaps they were planning some deviltry, but he could not divine the purpose of it. At any rate he was armed with his night stick and his trusty revolver. He had a clear space in which to protect himself, and he was not frightened by ghosts. So, alert though he was, his mind was not uneasy.

He turned casually, on his heels, to look up the Avenue. He was startled to see two stocky figures within five feet of him. That quick right-about had saved him from an attack, although he did not realize it. The approach of the men had been absolutely noiseless.

The rain beat down in his face, and the men hesitated an instant, as though interrupted in some plan. It did not occur to Burke that they had approached him with a purpose.

He looked at them sharply, by force of habit. Their evil faces showed pallid and grewsome in the flickering light of the arc-lamp on the corner by Shultberger's place.

The two men glared at him shrewdly, and then passed on by without a word. They walked half way down the block, and Burke, watching them from the corner of his eye, saw them cross the street and turn into the rear entrance of Shultberger's cabaret restaurant.

"Well, he's having some high-class callers to-night," mused Burke. "Perhaps he'll need a little help after all."

Even as he thought this he heard a crash of broken glass, and he turned abruptly toward the direction of the sound.

The arc-light had gone out.

Burke walked across the street and fumbled with his feet, feeling the broken glass which had showered down near the base of the pole.

"I wonder what happened to that lamp? They don't burst of their own accord like this generally."

He walked back to his position. The street was now very dark, because the nearest burning arc-lamp was half a block to the south. As Burke pondered on the situation he heard footsteps to his left. He turned about and a familiar voice greeted him. It was Patrolman Maguire.

"Well, Burke, your sins should sure be washed away in this deluge! I thought that I'd step up a minute and give you a chance to go get some dry clothes and a raincoat. You've another hour on the peg before I relieve you, but hustle down to the station house and rig yourself up, me lad."

It was a welcome cheery voice from the dismal night shades. But Burke objected to the suggestion.

"No, Maguire, I'll stick it out. I think there's trouble brewing, and it's only sixty more minutes. You keep on your patrol. We both might get a call-down for changing."

"Well, begorra, if there's any call-down for a little humanity, I don't give a rap. You go get some dry clothes. I know Cap. Sawyer won't mind. You can be back here in five minutes. You've done enough to-day to deserve a little consideration, me boy. Hustle now!"

Burke was chilled to the marrow and his teeth chattered, even though it was a Spring rain, and not the icy blasts of the earlier post nights.

"Well, keep a sharp lookout for this crowd around Shultberger's, Mack!"

He yielded, and turned toward the station house with a quick stride. He had hardly gone half a block before Maguire had reason to remember the warning. A cry of distress came from the vestibule of Shultberger's front entrance. The lights of the saloon had been suddenly extinguished.

"Sure, and that's some monkey business," thought Maguire, as he ran toward the doorway.

He pounded on the pavement with his night stick, and the resonant sound stopped Burke's retreat to the station. Officer 4434 wheeled about and ran for the post he had just left.

Maguire had barely reached the doorway of the saloon when a revolver shot rang out, and the red tongue licked his face.

"Now we got 'im!" cried a voice.

"Kill the rookie!"

"That's Burke, all right!"

Maguire felt a stinging sensation in his shoulder, and his nightstick dropped with a thud to the sidewalk. Three figures pounded upon him, and again the revolver spoke. This time there was no fault in the aim. A gallant Irish soul passed to its final goal as the weapon barked for the third time.

Burke's heart was in his mouth; it was no personal fear, but for the beloved comrade whom he felt sure had stepped into the fate intended for himself. He drew his revolver as he ran, and swung his stick from its leathern handle thong resoundingly on the sidewalk as he raced toward the direction of the scuffle.

A short figure darted out from a doorway as he approached the corner and deftly stuck a foot forward, tripping the policeman.

"Beat it, fellers!" called this adept, whose voice Burke recognized as that of Jimmie the Monk. It was a clever campaign which the gangsters had laid out, but their mistake in picking the man cost them dearly.

As he called, the Monk darted down the street for a quick escape, feeling confident that his enemy was lying dead in the doorway on the corner. Burke forgot the orders of the Mayor against the use of fire-arms; his mind inadvertently swung into the fighting mood of the old days in the Philippines, when native devils were dealt justice as befitted their own methods.

He had fallen heavily on the wet pavement, and slid. But, at the recognition of that evil voice, he rolled over, and half lying on the pavement he leveled his revolver at the fleeting figure of the gang leader.

Bang! One shot did the work, and Jimmie the Monk crumpled forward, with a leg which was never again to lead in another Bowery "spiel" or club prize fight.

"He's fixed," thought Burke, and he sprang up, to run forward to the vestibule of Shultberger's. There he found the body of Maguire sprawled out, with the blood of the Irish kings mingling with the rainwater on the East Side street.

One man was hiding in the doorway's shelter. Another was scuttling down the street, to run full into the arms of an approaching roundsman.

As Burke stooped over the form of his comrade a black-jack struck his shoulder. He sprang upward, partially numbed from the blow, but summoning all his strength he caught the gangster by the arm and shoulder and flung him bodily through the glass door which smashed with a clatter.

Burke kicked at the door as he fought with the murderer, and his weight forced it open.

A whisky bottle whizzed through the air from behind the bar. Shultberger was in the battle. Burke's night stick ended the struggle with his one assailant, and he ran for the long bar, which he vaulted, as the saloon-keeper dodged backward. Another revolver shot reverberated as the proprietor retreated. But, at this rough and tumble fight, Burke used the greatest fighting projectile of the policeman; he threw the loaded night stick with unerring aim, striking Shultberger full in the face. The man screamed as he fell backward.

Half a dozen policemen had surrounded the saloon by this time, and Burke fumbled around until he found the electric light switch near the cash register. He threw a flood of light on the scene of destruction.

Shultberger, pulling himself up to his knees, his face and mouth gory from the catapult's stroke, moaned with agony as he clawed blindly. Patrolman White was tugging at the gangster who had been knocked unconscious by Burke's club. Outside two of the uniformed men were reverently lifting the corpse of Terence Maguire, who was on his Eternal Fixed Post.

"Have ... have you sent ... for an ambulance?" cried Bobbie.

"Yes, Burke," said the sergeant, who had examined the dead man. "But it's too late. Poor Mack, poor old Mack!"

A patrol wagon was clanging its gong as the driver spurred the horses on. Captain Sawyer dismounted from the seat by the driver. The bad news had traveled rapidly. Suddenly Burke, remembering the fleeing Jimmie, dashed from the saloon, and forced his way through the swarming crowd which had been drawn from the neighboring tenements by the excitement.

"Is the boy crazy?" asked Sawyer. "Hurry, White, and notify the Coroner, for I don't intend to allow Terence Maguire to lie in this rotten den very long."

Burke ran along the wet street, looking vainly for the wounded gang-leader. Jimmie was not in sight! Burke went the entire length of the block, and then slowly retraced his steps.

He scrutinized every hallway and cellar entrance.

At last his vigilance was rewarded. Down the steps, beneath a half-opened bulkhead door, he found his quarry.

The Monk was moaning with pain from a shattered leg-bone.

Burke clambered down and tried to lift the wounded man.

"Get up here!" he commanded.

"Oh, dey didn't get ye, after all!" cried Jimmie, recognizing his voice. He sank his teeth in the hand which was stretched forth to help him. Burke swung his left hand, still numb from the black-jack blow on his shoulder, and caught the ruffian's nose and forehead. A vigorous pull drew the fellow's teeth loose with a jerk.

"Well, you dog!" grunted the policeman, as he dragged the gangster to the street level. "You'll have iron bars to bite before many hours, and then the electric chair!"

Jimmie's nerve went back on him.

"Oh, Gaud! Dey can't do dat! I didn't do it. I wasn't dere!"

Burke said nothing, but holding the man down to the pavement with a knee on his back, he whistled for the patrol wagon.

The prisoners were soon arraigned, Shultberger, Jimmie the Monk and the first gangster were sent to the hospital shortly after under guard. The second runner, who had been caught by White, was searched, and by comparison of the weapons and the empty chambers of each one the police deduced that it was he who had fired the shots which killed Maguire. The entire band, including the saloon-keeper, were equally guilty before the law, and their trial and sentencing to pay the penalty were assured.

But back in the station house, late that night, the thought of punishment brought little consolation to a heart-broken corps of policemen.

Big, husky men sobbed like women. Death on duty was no stranger in their lives; but the loss of rollicking, generous Maguire was a bitter shock just the same.

And next morning, as Burke read the papers, after a wretched, sleepless night, he saw the customary fifteen line article, headed: "ANOTHER POLICEMAN MURDERED BY GANGSTERS." Five million fellow New Yorkers doubtless saw the brief story as well, and passed it by to read the baseball gossip, the divorce news, or the stock quotations—without a fleeting thought of regret.

It was just the same old story, you know.

Had it been the story of a political boss's beer-party to the bums of his ward; had it been an account of Mrs. Van Astorbilt's elopement with a plumber; had it been the life-story of a shooting show girl; had it been the description of the latest style in slit skirts; had it been a sarcastic message from some drunken, over-rated city official; had it been a sympathy-squad description of the hardships and soul-beauties of a millionaire murderer it would have met with close attention.

But what is so stale as the oft-told, ever-old yarn of a policeman's death?

"What do we pay them for?"

CHAPTER XIII

LORNA'S QUEST FOR PLEASURE

In the same morning papers Burke saw lengthy notices of the engagement of Miss Sylvia Trubus, only child of William Trubus, the famous philanthropist, to Ralph Gresham, the millionaire manufacturer of electrical machinery.

"There, that should interest Mr. Barton. His ex-employer is marrying into a very good family, to put it mildly, and Trubus will have a very rich son-in-law! I wonder if she'll be as happy as I intend to make Mary when she says the word?"

He cut one of the articles out of the paper, putting it into his pocket to show Mary that evening. He had a wearing and sorrowful day; his testimony was important for the arraignment of the dozen or more criminals who had been rounded up through his efforts during the preceding twenty-four hours. The gloom of Maguire's death held him in its pall throughout the day in court.

He hurried uptown to meet Mary as she left the big confectionery store at closing time.

Mary had been busy and worried through the day. At noon she had gone to the station to bid goodbye to Henrietta Bailey, who was now well on her way to the old town and Joe.

As the working day drew to a close Mary was kept busy filling a large order for a kindly faced society woman and her pretty daughter.

"You have waited on me several times before," she told Mary, "and you have such good taste. I want the very cutest bon-bons and favors, and they must be delivered up on Riverside Drive to our house in time for dinner. You know my daughter's engagement was announced in the papers to-day, while we had intended to let it be a surprise at a big dinner party to-night. Well, the dear girl is very happy, and I want this dinner to give her one of the sweetest memories of her life."

Mary entered into the spirit with zest, and being a clever saleswoman, she collected a wonderful assortment of dainty novelties and confections, while the manager of the store rubbed his hands together gleefully as he observed the correspondingly wonderful size of the bill.

"There, that should help the jollity along," said Mary. "I hope I have pleased you. I envy your daughter, not for the candies and the dinner, but for having such a mother. My mother has been dead for years."

The tears welled into her eyes, and the customer smiled tenderly at her.

"You are a dear girl, and if ever I have the chance to help you I will; don't forget it. I am so happy myself; perhaps selfishly so. But my life has been along such even lines, such a wonderful husband, and such a daughter. I am so proud of her. She is marrying a young man who is very rich, yet with a strong character, and he will make her very happy I am sure. Well, dear, I will give you my address, for I wish you would see personally that these goodies are delivered to us without delay."

Mary took her pad and pencil.

"Mrs. William Trubus—Riverside Drive."

The girl's expression was curious; she remembered Bobbie's description of the husband. It hardly seemed possible that such a man could be blessed with so sweet a wife and daughter—but such undeserved blessings seem too often to be the unusual injustice of Fate in this twisted, tangled old world, as Mary well knew.

"All right, Mrs. Trubus; I shall follow your instructions and will go to the delivery room myself to see that they are sent out immediately."

"Good afternoon, my dear," and Mrs. Trubus and her happy daughter left the store.

Mary was as good as her word, and she made sure that the several parcels were on their way to Riverside Drive before she returned to the front of the store. When she did so she saw a little tableau, unobserved by the busy clerks and customers, which made her heart stand still.

Lorna was standing by one of the bon-bon show cases talking to a tall stranger who ogled her in bold fashion, and a manner which indicated that the conversation was far from that of business.

"Who can that be?" thought Mary. An intuition of danger crept over her as she watched the shades of sinister suggestion on the face of the man who whispered to her sister.

The man was urging, Lorna half-protesting, as though refusing some enticing offer.

Mary stepped closer, and the deep tones of the stranger's voice filled her with a thrill of loathing. It was a voice which she felt she could never forget as long as she lived.

THE DEEP TONES OF THE STRANGER'S VOICE FILLED MARY WITH A THRILL OF LOATHING.   p. 227

The deep tones of the stranger's voice filled her with a thrill of loathing.

"Come up to my office with me when you finish work and I'll book you up this very evening. The show will open in two weeks, and I will give you a speaking part, maybe even one song to sing. You know I'm strong for you, little girl, and always have been. My influence counts a lot—and you know influence is the main thing for a successful actress!"

Mary could stand it no longer.

She touched Lorna on the arm, and the younger girl turned around guiltily, her eyes dropping as she saw her sister's stern questioning look.

"Who is this man, Lorna?"

The stranger smiled, and threw his head back defiantly.

"A friend of mine."

"What does he want?"

"That is none of your affair, Mary."

"It is my affair. You are employed here to work, not to talk with men nor to flirt. You had better attend to your work. And, as for you, I shall complain to the manager if you don't get out of here at once!"

The stranger laughed softly, but there was a brutal twitch to his jaw as he retorted: "I'm a customer here, and I guess the manager won't complain if I spend money. Here, little girlie, pick me out a nice box of chocolates. The

- 117 -

most expensive you have. I'm going to take my sweetheart out to dinner, and I am a man who spends his money right. I'm not a cheap policeman!"

Mary's face paled.

Her blood boiled, and only the breeding of generations of gentlewomen restrained her from slapping the man's face. She watched Lorna, who could not restrain a giggle, as she took down a be-ribboned candy box, and began to fill it with chocolate dainties.

"Oh, if Bobbie were only here!" thought Mary in despair. "This man is a villain. It is he who has been filling Lorna's mind with stage talk. I don't believe he is a theatrical man, either. They would not insult me so!"

The manager bustled about.

"Closing time, girls. Get everything orderly now, and hurry up. You know, the boss has been kicking about the waste light bills which you girls run up in getting things straight at the end of the day."

Mary turned to her own particular counter, and she saw the big man leave the store, as the manager obsequiously bowed him out.

In the wardrobe room where they kept their wraps, Mary took Lorna aside. Her eyes were flaming orbs, as she laid a trembling hand upon the girl's arm.

"Lorna, you are not going to that man's office?"

"Oh, not right away," responded her sister airily. "We are going to Martin's first for a little dinner, and maybe a tango or two. What's that to you, Mary? Stick to your policeman."

Mary dropped her hand weakly. She put on her hat and street-coat, hardly knowing what she was doing.

"Oh, Lorna, child, you are so mistaken, so weak," she began.

"I'm not weak, nor foolish. A girl can't live decently on the money they pay in this place. I'm going to show how strong I am by earning a real salary. I can get a hundred a week on the stage with my looks, and my voice, and my ... figure...."

In spite of her bravado she hesitated at the last word. It was a little daring, even to her, and she was forcing a bold front to maintain her own determination, for the girl had hesitated at the man's pleadings until her sister's interference had piqued her into obstinacy.

"It won't hurt to find out how much I can get, even if I don't take the offer at all," Lorna thought. "I simply will not submit to Mary's dictation all the time."

Lorna hurried to the street, closely followed by her sister.

"Don't go, dear," pleaded Mary.

But there by the curb panted a big limousine, such as Lorna had always pictured waiting for her at a stage door; the big man smiled as he held open the door. Lorna hesitated an instant. Then she espied, coming around the corner toward them, Bobbie Burke, on his way to meet Mary.

That settled it. She ran with a laugh toward the door of the automobile and flounced inside, while the big man followed her, slamming the portal as the car moved on.

"Oh, Bob," sobbed Mary, as the young officer reached her side. "Follow them."

"What's the matter?"

"Look, that black automobile!"

"Yes, yes!"

"Lorna has gone into it with a theatrical manager. She is going on the stage!" and Mary caught his hand tensely as she dashed after the car.

It was a hopeless pursuit, for another machine had already come between them. It was impossible for Burke to see the number of the car, and then it turned around the next corner and was lost in the heavy traffic.

"Oh, what are we to do?" exclaimed Mary in despair.

"Well, we can go to all the theatrical offices, and make inquiries. I have my badge under my coat, and they will answer, all right."

They went to every big office in the whole theatrical district. But there, too, the search was vain. Mary was too nervous and wretched to enjoy the possibility of a dinner, and so Burke took her home. Her father asked for Lorna, to which Mary made some weak excuse which temporarily quieted the old gentleman.

Promising to keep up his search in restaurants and offices, Burke hurried on downtown again. It was useless. Throughout the night he sought, but no trace of the girl had been found. When he finally went up to the Barton home to learn if the young girl had returned, he found the old man frantic with fear and worriment.

"Burke, some ill has befallen the child," he exclaimed. "Mary has finally told me the truth, and my heart is breaking."

"There, sir, you must be patient. We will try our best. I can start an investigation through police channels that will help along."

"But father became so worried that we called up your station. The officer at the other end of the telephone took the name, and said he would send out a notice to all the stations to start a search."

"Great Scott! That means publicity, Miss Mary. The papers will have the story sure, now. There have been so many cases of girls disappearing lately that they are just eager for another to write up."

Mary wrung her hands, and the old man chattered on excitedly.

"Then if it is publicity I don't care. I want my daughter, and I will do everything in the world to get her."

Burke calmed them as much as he could, but if ever two people were frantic with grief it was that unhappy pair.

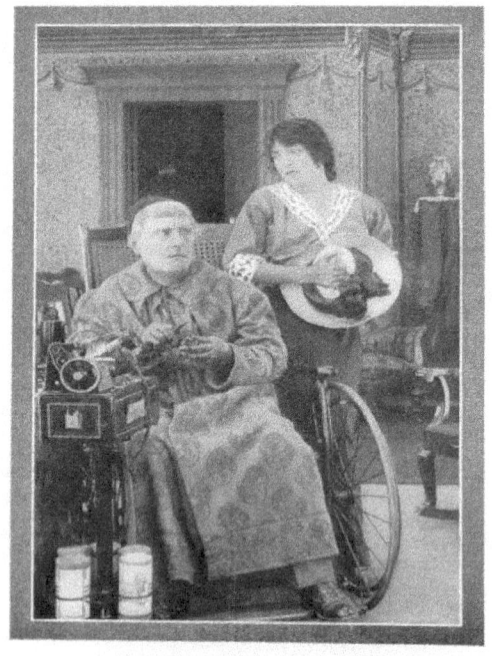

Father and daughter were frantic with grief.

Bobbie hurried on downtown again, promising to keep them advised about the situation.

After he left Mary went to her own room, and by the side of the bed which she and the absent one had shared so long, she knelt to ask for stronger aid than any human being could give.

If ever prayer came from the depths of a broken heart, it was that forlorn plea for the lost sister!

All through the night they waited in vain.

The first page of every New York paper carried the sensational story of the disappearance of Lorna Barton. Not that such a happening was unusual, but in view of the white slavery arrests and the gang fight in which Bobbie Burke had figured so prominently; his partial connection with the case, and those details which the fertile-minded reporters could fill in, it was full of human interest, and "yellow" as the heart of any editor could desire.

Pale and heart-sick Mary went down to Monnarde's next morning. The girls crowded about her in the wardrobe room, some to express real sympathy, others to show their condescension to one whom they inwardly felt was far superior in manners, appearance and ability.

Mary thanked them, and dry-eyed went to her place behind the counter. For reasons best known to himself, the manager was late in arriving that morning. The minutes seemed century-long to Mary as she hoped against hope.

A surprisingly early customer was Mrs. Trubus, who came hurrying in from her big automobile. She went to Mary's counter and observed the girl's demeanor.

"Dear, was it your sister that I read about in the paper this morning?" she inquired.

"Yes," very meekly. Mary tried to hold back the tears which seemed so near the surface.

"I am so sorry. I remembered that you once spoke of your sister when you were waiting on me. The paper said that she worked here at Monnarde's, and I remembered my promise of yesterday that I would do anything for you that I could. Mr. Trubus is greatly interested in philanthropic work, and of course what I could do would be very small in comparison to his influence. But if there is a single thing...."

"There's not, I'm afraid. Oh, I'm so miserable—and my poor dear old daddy!"

Even as she spoke the manager came bustling into the store. He had evidently passed an uncomfortable night himself, although from an entirely different cause. In his hand he bore the morning paper, which he just bought outside the door from one of several newsboys who stood there shouting about the "candy store mystery," as one paper had headlined it.

"See, here!" cried he, turning to Mary at once. "What do you mean by bringing this disgrace down upon the most fashionable candy shop in New York. You will ruin our business."

"Oh, Mr. Fleming," began Mary brokenly, "I don't understand what you mean. I have done nothing, sir!"

"Nothing! *Nothing*! You and this miserable sister of yours! Complaining to the police, are you, about men flirting with the girls in my store? Do you think society women want to come to a shop where the girls flirt with customers? No! I'm done right now. Get your hat and get out of here!"

"Why, what do you mean?" gasped the girl, her fingers contracting and twitching nervously.

"You're fired—bounced—ousted!" he cried. "That's what I mean." He turned toward the other girls and in a strident voice, unmindful of the two or three customers in the place, continued. "Let this be a lesson. I will discharge every girl in the place if I see her flirting. The idea!"

And he pompously walked back to his office as important as a toad in a lonely puddle.

Mary turned to the counter, which she caught for support. One of the girls ran to her, but Mrs. Trubus, standing close by, placed a motherly arm about her waist.

"There, you poor dear. Don't you despair. This is a large world, and there are more places for an honest, clever girl to work in than a candy store run by a popinjay! You get your hat and get right into my car, and I will take you down to my husband's office, and see what we can do there. Come right along, now, with me."

"Oh, I must go home!" murmured Mary brokenly.

But at the elderly woman's insistence she walked back, unsteadily, to the wardrobe room for her hat and coat.

"How dare you walk out the front way," raved the manager, as she was leaving with Mrs. Trubus.

Mary did not hear him. The tears, a blessed relief, were coursing down her flower-white cheeks as the kindly woman steadied her arm.

"Well! That suits me well enough," muttered Mr. Fleming philosophically, as he retired to his private office. "I lost a lot at poker last night—and here are two salaries for almost a full week that won't go into anyone's pockets but my own. First, last and always, a business man, say I."

CHAPTER XIV

CHARITY AND THE MULTITUDE OF SINS

In the outer office of William Trubus an amiable little scene was being enacted, far different from the harrowing ones which had made up the last twelve hours for poor Mary.

Miss Emerson, the telephone girl, was engaged in animated repartee with that financial genius of the "Mercantile Agency," with whose workings the reader may have a slight familiarity, located on the floor below of the same Fifth Avenue building.

"Yes, dearie, during business hours I'm as hard as nails, but when I shut up my desk I'm just as good a fellow as the next one. All work and no play gathers no moss," remarked Mr. John Clemm.

"You're a comical fellow, Mr. Clemm. I'd just love to go out to-night, as you suggest. And if you've got a gent acquaintance who is like you, I have the swellest little lady friend you ever seen. Her name is Clarice, and she is a manicure girl at the Astor. We might have a foursome, you know."

"That's right, girlie," responded Clemm, as he ingratiatingly placed an arm about her wasp-like waist. "But two's company, and four's too much of a corporation for me."

"Oh, Mr. Clemm—nix on this in here—Mr. Trubus is in his office, and he'll get wise...."

As she spoke, not Mr. Trubus, but his estimable wife interrupted the progress of the courtship. She walked into the doorway, from the elevator corridor, holding Mary's arm.

As she saw the lover-like attitude of the plump Mr. Clemm, she gasped, and then burst out in righteous indignation.

"Why, you shameless girl, what do you mean by such actions in the office of the Purity League? I shall tell my husband at once!"

Miss Emerson sprang away from the amorous entanglement with Mr. Clemm and tried to say something. She could think of nothing which befitted the occasion; all her glib eloquence was temporarily asphyxiated. Mr. Clemm stammered and looked about for some hole in which to conceal himself. He, too, seemed far different from the pugnacious, self-confident dictator who reigned supreme on the floor below.

"William! William Trubus!" called the philanthropist's wife angrily. Her husband heard from within, and he opened the door with a thoroughly startled look.

"My dear wife!" he began, purring and somewhat uncertain as to the cause of the trouble. Mary, nervous as she was, observed a curious interchange of glances between the two men.

"William, I find this brazen creature standing here hugging this man, as though your office, the Purity League's headquarters, were some Lover's Lane! It is disgusting."

"Well, well, my dear," stammered Trubus. "Don't be too harsh."

"I am not harsh, but I have too much respect for you and the high ideals for which I know you battle every hour of the day to endure such a thing. Suppose the Bishop had come in instead of myself? Would he consider such actions creditable to the great purpose for which the church takes up collections twice each year throughout his diocese?"

Trubus tilted back and forth on his toes and tapped the ends of his plump fingers together. He was sparring for time. The girl looked at him saucily, and the offending visitor shrugged his shoulders as he quietly started for the door.

"Tut, tut, my dear! I shall reprimand the girl."

"You shall discharge her at once!" insisted Mrs. Trubus, her eyes flashing. "She will disgrace the office and the great cause."

Trubus was in a quandary. He looked about him. Miss Emerson, with a confident smile, walked toward the general office on the left.

"I should worry about this job. I'm sick of this charity stuff anyway. I'm going to get a cinch job with a swell broker I know. He runs a lot of bunco games, too—but he admits. Don't let the old lady worry about me, Mr. Trubus, but don't forget that I've got two weeks' salary coming to me. And you just raised my weekly insult to twenty-five dollars last Saturday, you know, Mr. Trubus."

With this Parthian shot, she slammed the door of the general stenographers' room, and left Mr. Trubus to face his irate wife.

"You pay that girl twenty-five dollars for attending to a telephone, William? Why, that's more money than you earned when we had been married ten years. Twenty-five dollars a week for a telephone girl!"

"There, my dear, it is quite natural. She is especially tactful and worth it," said Trubus, in embarrassment. "You are not exactly tactful yourself, my dear, to nag me in front of an employee. As the Scriptures say, a gentle wife...."

Mrs. Trubus gave the philanthropist one deep look which seemed to cause aphasia on the remainder of the Scriptural quotation.

For the first time Trubus noticed Mary Barton, standing in embarrassed silence by the door, wishing that she could escape from the scene.

"Who is this young person, my dear?"

"This is a young girl who is in deep trouble, and without a position through no fault of her own. I brought her down to your office to have you help her, William."

"But, alas, our finances are so low that we have no room for any additional office force," began Trubus.

"There, that will do. If you pay twenty-five dollars a week to the telephone operator no wonder the finances are low. You have just discharged her, and I insist on your giving this young lady an opportunity."

Trubus reddened, and tried to object.

But his good wife overruled him.

"Have you ever used a switchboard, miss?" he began.

"Yes, sir. In my last position I began on the switchboard, and worked that way for nearly two months. I am sure I can do it."

Trubus did not seem so optimistic. But, at his wife's silent argument—looks more eloquent than a half hour of oratory, he nodded grudgingly.

"Well, you can start in. Just hang your hat over on the wall hook. Come into my office, my dear wife."

They entered, and Mary sat down, still in a daze. She had been so suddenly discharged and then employed again that it seemed a dream. Even the terrible hours of the night seemed some hideous nightmare rather than reality.

Miss Emerson came from the side room, attired in a street garb which would have brought envy to many a chorus girl.

"Oh, my dear, and so you are to follow my job. Well, I wish you joy, sweetie. Tell Papa Trubus that I'll be back after lunch time for my check. And keep your lamps rolling on the old gink and he'll raise your salary once a month. He's not such a dead one if he is strong on this charity game. Life with Trubus is just one telephone girl after another ... ta, ta, dearie. I'm off stage."

And she departed, leaving simple Mary decidedly mystified by her diatribe.

A few minutes brought another diversion. This time it was Sylvia Trubus and Ralph Gresham, her fiancé, come for a call.

"Is my father in?" she asked, absorbed in the well groomed, selfish young man. Mary rang the private bell and announced Miss Trubus. Her father hurried to the door, and when he saw his prospective son-in-law his face wreathed in smiles.

"Ah, Mr. Gresham, Ralph, I might say, I am delighted! Come right in!"

Mary was startled as she heard the name of the young girl's sweetheart.

"I'm afraid that she will not be as happy as she thinks, if daddy has told me right about Ralph Gresham. But, oh, if I could hear something from Bobbie about Lorna. I believe I will call him up."

She was just summoning the courage for a private call when the private office door opened, and Gresham, Sylvia, her mother and Trubus emerged.

"I will return in ten minutes, Miss," said Trubus. "If there are any calls just take a record of them. Allow no one to go into my private office."

"Yes, sir."

Mary waited patiently for a few moments, when suddenly a telephone bell began to jangle inside the private office.

"That's curious," she murmured, looking at her own key-board. "There's no connection." Again she heard it, insistent, yet muffled.

She walked to the door and opened it. As she did so the wind blew in from the open casement, making a strong draught. Half a dozen papers blew from Trubus' desk to the floor. Frightened lest her inquisitiveness should cause trouble, Mary hurriedly stooped and picked up the papers, carrying them back to the desk. As she leaned over it she noticed a curious little metal box, glass-covered. Under this glass an automatic pencil was writing by electrical connection.

"What on earth can that be?" she wondered. The bell tinkled, in its muffled way, once more.

The moving pencil went on. She watched it, fascinated, even at the risk of being caught, hardly realizing that she was doing what might be termed a dishonorable act.

"Paid Sawyer $250. Girl safe, but still unconscious."

Mary's heart beat suddenly. The thought of her own sister was so burdensome upon her own mind that the mention by this mysterious communication of a girl, "safe but still unconscious," strung her nerves as though with an electric shock. She leaned over the little recording instrument, which was built on a hinged shelf that could be cunningly swung into the desk body, and covered with a false front. As she did so she saw a curious little instrument, shaped somewhat like the receiver of a telephone receiver. Mary's experience with her father's work told her what that instrument was.

"A dictagraph!" she exclaimed.

Instinctively she picked it up, and heard a conversation which was so startling in its import to herself that her heart seemed to congeal for an instant.

"I tell you, Jack, the girl is still absolutely out of it. We can risk shipping her anywhere the way she is now. I chloroformed her in the auto as soon as we got away from the candy store. But that Burke nearly had us, for I saw him coming."

"You will have to dispose of her to-day, Shepard. Give her some strong coffee—a good stiff needleful of cocaine will bring her around. Do something, that's all, or you don't get a red cent of the remaining three hundred. Now, I'm a busy man. You'll have to talk louder, too, my hearing isn't what it used to be."

"Say, Clemm, quit this kidding about your ears. I've tried you out and you can hear better than I can. There's some game you're working on me and if there is, I'll...."

"Can the tragedy, Shepard. Save it for that famous whipping stunt of yours. Beat this girl up a bit, and tell me where she is."

"I'll do that in an hour, and not a minute sooner, and I've got to have the other three hundred."

Mary dropped the receiver. She wanted to know where that conversation could come from. Down the side of the desk she traced a delicate wire. Under the rug it went, and across to the window. She looked out. A fire escape passed the window. It was open. She saw the little wire cross through the woodwork to the outside brick construction and down the wall. Softly she clambered down the fire-escape until she could peer through the window on the floor below.

There at a desk, in the private office of the "Mercantile" association, sat the man who had been hugging her predecessor at Trubus' switchboard, the man who had exchanged the curious looks with the philanthropist. Talking to him was the man who had taken her sister away from the candy store the day before!

Hurriedly she climbed back up the fire escape into the window, out through the door of the private office, closing it behind her.

She telephoned Bobbie at the station house. Fortunately he was there. She gave him her address, and before he could express his surprise begged him to hurry to the doorway of the building and wait for her.

He promised.

Mary kept her nerves as quiet as she could, praying that the man Sawyer would not leave before she could follow him with Bobbie. In a few minutes one of the girls from the stenography room came out. Seeing that she was the new girl the young woman spoke: "Do you want me to relieve you while you go to lunch. I'm not going out to-day. I'm so glad to see anyone here but that fresh Miss Emerson that it will be a pleasure."

"Thank you. I do want to go now," said Mary nervously. She hurriedly donned her hat and rushed down to the street. Bobbie was waiting for her, as he had lost not a minute.

They waited behind the big door column for several minutes. Suddenly a man came swinging through the portal. It was Sawyer.

Bobbie remembered him instantly, while Mary gripped his arm until she pinched it.

"We'll follow him," said Burke, for the girl had already told of the dictagraph conversation.

Follow him they did. Up one street and down another. At last the man led them over into Burke's own precinct. He ascended the iron steps of an old-fashioned house which had once been a splendid mansion in generations gone by.

"Ah, that's where Lorna is hidden, as sure as you're standing here, Mary. From what he said no harm has come to her yet. Hurry with me to the station house, and we'll have the reserves go through that house in a jiffy."

It took not more than ten minutes for the police to surround the house. But disappointment was their only reward. Somehow or other the rascals had received a tip of premonition of trouble; perhaps Shepard was suspicious of his principals, and wished to move the girl out of their reach.

The house was empty, except for a few pieces of furniture.

"Look!" cried Mary, as she went through the rooms with Bob. "There is a handkerchief. She snatched it up. It was one of her own, with the initials "M. B." in a monogram.

"Lorna has been here," she exclaimed. "I remember handing her that very handkerchief when we were in the store yesterday."

"What's to be done now?" thought Bobbie. "We had better go up to your father and tell him what we know—it is not as bad as it might have been."

"Precious little comfort," sighed Mary, exhausted beyond tears.

They reached the desolate home, and Bob broke the news to the old man. As Mary poured forth her story of the discovery in Trubus' office, her father's face lighted with renewed hope.

To their surprise he laughed, softly, and then spoke:

"Mary, my child, my long hours of study and labor on my own invention have not been in vain. My dictagraph-recorder—this very model here, which I have just completed shall be put to its first great test to save my own daughter. Heaven could reward me in no more wonderful manner than to let it help in the rescue of little Lorna—why did I not think of it sooner?"

"What shall we do, father?" breathlessly cried Mary.

"Can I help, Mr. Barton?"

"Describe the arrangement of the offices."

Mary rapidly limned the plan of the headquarters of the Purity League. Her father nodded and his lips moved as he repeated her words in a whisper.

"I have it now. You must put the instrument under the telephone switchboard table," he directed. "Pile up a waste-basket, or something that is handy to keep it out of view. I have already adjusted enough fresh cylinders to record at least one hour of conversation. This machine is run by an automatic spring, which you must wind like a clock. Here I will wind it myself to have all in readiness."

He rolled his chair swiftly to his work table, and turned the little crank, continuing his plan of attack.

"Now, take the long wire, and run it through the door of the private office up close to the desk. Attach this disc to the dictagraph receiver. It is so small, and the wiring so fine that it will not be noticed if it is done correctly. Here, Burke. I will do it now to this loose dictagraph receiver. Watch me."

The old man worked swiftly.

Burke scrutinized each move, and nodded in understanding.

"Be careful to cover the wire along the floor with a rug—he must never be allowed to see that, you know. After you have all this prepared, Mary, you must start the mechanism going, and then get the reproduction of the conversation as it comes on the dictagraph."

"All right, father—but how shall we get it there without Mr. Trubus knowing about it? He is very watchful of that room."

Barton patted Bobbie's broad shoulder, with a confident smile.

"I think Officer 4434 can devise a way for that. He has had harder tasks and won out. Now, hurry down with the machine. It is a bit heavy. You had better take it in a taxicab. You will spend all your money on taxicabs, my boy, I am afraid."

"Well, sir, a little money now isn't important enough to worry about if it means happiness for the future—for us all."

Mary's face reddened, and she dropped her eyes. There was an understanding between the three which needed no words for explanation. So it is that the sweetest love creeps into its final nestling place.

"God bless you, my boy. I'm an old man and none too good, but I shall pray for your success."

"Good bye," said Bobbie, as he and Mary left with the mechanism.

Bobbie stopped the taxicab which carried them half a block east of the office building which was their goal.

"Mary, I will take this machine up on the floor above Trubus' office, and hide it in the hall. Then you go to your place in the office and I will manage a way to draw Mr. Trubus out in a hurry. We will work together after that, and spread the electric trap for him."

Mary went direct to the office, where she found Trubus storming about angrily.

"What do you mean by staying nearly two hours out at luncheon time?" he cried. "I am very busy and I want you to be here on duty regularly, even if my wife did foolishly intercede in your behalf, young woman."

"I am sorry—I became ill, and was delayed. I will not be late with you again, sir."

The president of the Purity League retired to his sanctum, slightly mollified. Mary had not been at her post long when a messenger came in with a telegram.

"Mr. Trubus!" he said, shoving the envelope at her.

She signed his book, and knocked at the door. There was a little delay, and the worthy man opened it impatiently. "I do not want to be interrupted, I am going over my accounts."

She handed him the telegram, and he tore it open hastily.

"What's this?" he muttered in excitement. Then he went back for his silk hat, and left, slamming the door of his private office and carefully locking it.

"I wonder what took him out so quickly?" thought Mary. But even as she mused Bobbie Burke came into the outer office, with the precious machine wrapped in yellow paper.

"What took Trubus out, Bobbie?" she asked, as she helped him arrange the machine behind the wastebasket, near the telephone switchboard.

"Just a telegram, signed 'Friend,' advising him to watch the men who came in the front door, downstairs, for ten minutes, but not to visit Clemm's office. That will keep him away, and he can't possibly guess who did it."

"But, look, Bob, he has locked his door with a peculiar key. If you force it he will be able to tell."

"I thought he might do as much, Mary. I wouldn't risk tampering with the lock. Instead, I found an empty room on the floor above. I have a rope, and I will take the receiver of your father's machine with the disc, and part of the wiring which I had already cut. There is no fire escape from the floor above for some reason. He will suspect all the less, then, for he would not think of anyone coming through the headquarters on the floor below. I will go down hand over hand, you shove the wire under the door to me, and I'll attach it. Then I'll go up the ladder, and we'll let the dictagraph do its work."

Thus it was accomplished. Mary covered the machine and its wiring in the outer office, although several times she had to quit at inopportune times to answer the telephone, or make a connection.

Burke, from the room above, climbed down hurriedly, adjusted the instrument as he had been told to do by John Barton. Then he was out, barely drawing himself and the rope away from the window view before Trubus entered.

Mary thought that it was all discovered, but breathed a sigh of relief when the president opened the door and entered without a remark.

It was lucky for Burke that the day was so warm, for the president had left the window open when he left, otherwise Burke could not possibly have carried out his plan so opportunely.

The telephone bell rang. Mary answered and was greeted by Bob's voice.

"Is it you, Mary?" he exclaimed hurriedly.

"Yes."

"Then start your machine, for I saw this man Shepard go upstairs to the floor beneath you."

"All right, Bob," said Mary softly.

"When the records are run out, unless I telephone you sooner, call one of the girls to take your place, tell her you are sick, and smuggle out the records—don't bother about the machine, we'll get that later. I will be downstairs waiting for you."

"Yes. I understand."

The time dragged horribly, but at last the hour had passed, and Mary wrapped up the precious wax cylinders and hurried downstairs.

Bob was pacing up and down anxiously.

"Shepard has eluded me. I was afraid to leave you, and he took an auto, and disappeared over toward the East Side. I have telephoned Captain Sawyer to have a phonograph ready for us. Come, we'll get over to the station at once. I hope your records give us the clue. If they don't, I'm afraid the trail is lost."

They hurried to the station house. In the private office of the Captain they found that officer waiting with eagerness.

"What's it all about, Bob?" he cried. "Why this phonograph?"

"It will explain itself, Captain," answered 4434. "Let's fix these records in the regular way, and then we will run them in order."

They did so in absolute silence. The Captain listened, first in bewilderment, then in great excitement.

"Great snakes! Where did you get those? That is a conversation between a bunch of traffickers. Listen, they are buying and selling, making reports and laying out their work for the night."

"Sssh!" cautioned Bob. "There's something important we want to get."

Suddenly Mary gripped his hand.

"That's Shepard's voice. I'd never forget it."

They listened. The man told of the condition of Lorna, mentioning her by name now. She had returned to consciousness, and was detained in the room of a house not five blocks from the police station.

"I'll break her spirit now. None of this stage talk any more, Clemm," droned the voice in the phonograph. "When I get my whip going she'll be glad enough to put on the silk dresses. She screamed and cried a while ago, but I'm used to that sort of guff."

"Don't mark her up with the whip, Shepard. That's a weakness of yours, and makes us lose money. Go over now and get her ready for to-night. They want a girl like her for a party up-town to-night. Get her scared, and then slip a little cocaine,—that eases 'em up. Then some champagne, and it will be easy."

Mary began to sob. Burke held her hand in his firm manner.

"Don't cry, little girl, we'll attend to her. Captain Sawyer, this is a record of a conversation we took on a new machine in the offices of the Purity League. It connects with the 'Mercantile' office downstairs, which is a headquarters for the white slave business. Now we know the address of the house where this young girl is kept. Can I have the reserves to help me raid it?"

"Ah, can you? Why, you will lead it my boy. Run out and order four machines from that garage next door. We'll be there in two minutes."

The reserves were summoned from their lounging room with such speed that Mary was bewildered.

"Oh, may I go along?" she begged. "I want to be the first to greet my little sister."

"Yes!" cried Sawyer. "All out now, boys. We'll work this on time. I know the house. It has a big back yard, and a fire-escape in the rear. Half you fellows follow the sergeant, and go to the front—but stay down by the corner until exactly four-thirty. Then break into the front door with axes. The other half—you men in that second file" (they were lined up with military precision in the big room of the station house)—"go with Bob Burke. I want you to go up over the roof. Use your night sticks if there is any gun play, shoot—but not to kill, for we want to send these men to prison."

They started off. Mary's heart fluttered with excitement, with hope. There was something so reassuring about the husky manhood of these blue-coats and the nonchalance and even delight with which they faced the dangers before them.

"Can I go in with them?" she cried eagerly.

"No, young lady, you stay with the sergeant, and sit in the automobile when the men leave it. You're apt to get shot, and we want you to take care of your sister."

They were off on the race to save Lorna!

Now the machines sped down the street. They separated at one thoroughfare, and the men with Burke went down another street to approach the house from the rear. This they did, quietly but rapidly, through the basement of an old house whose frightened tenants feared that they were to be arrested and lynched on the spot, to judge from their terror.

"Keep quiet," said Burke, "and don't look out of the windows, or we will arrest you."

Burke and his men peered at the building which was the object of their attack. The fire escape came only down to the second story.

"Well, you fellows will have to give me a boost, and I'll jump for the lower rungs. Then toss up one more man and I'll catch his hand. We can go up together. You watch the doors."

At exactly four thirty they dashed across the yard, scrambled over the fence, and like Zouaves in an exhibition drill, tossed Burke up to the lowest iron bar of the fire escape. He failed the first time. He tumbled back upon them. The second time was successful. Patrolman White was given a lift and Burke helped to pull him upon the fire-escape.

"Up, now, White! We will be behind the other fellows in the front!"

They lost not a second. It was an ape-like climb, but the two trained athletes made it in surprising time.

As they reached the top of the building a man scrambled out of the trap which led from the skylight.

"Grab him," yelled Burke.

White did so. This was prisoner number one.

Down the ladder, through the opening Burke went and found himself in a dingy garret, at the top of a rickety stair-case. He heard screams. He descended the steps half a floor and peering from the angle, through the transom of a room which led from the hall, he saw a fat old woman standing with her hands on her hips, laughing merrily, while Shepard was swinging a whip upon the shoulders of a screaming girl. Her clothes were half torn from her back, and the whip left a red welt each time it struck.

Downstairs Burke heard the crashing of breaking doors. The raid was progressing rapidly. Burke dashed down to the floor level and flung himself upon the locked door. The first lunge cracked the lock. The second swung the door back on its hinges.

He half fell into the room.

As he did so Lorna Barton saw him and in a flash of recognition, screamed: "Oh, save me, Mr. Burke!"

She staggered forward, and Shepard missed his aim, striking the fat woman who squealed with pain.

"I've got *you* now!" cried Burke, rushing for the ruffian with his stick.

"No, you haven't!" hissed Shepard, a fighting animal to the last. He had whipped out a magazine gun from his coat pocket, and began firing point-blank. Burke threw his stick at the man, but it went wild.

His own revolver was out now, and he sent a bullet into the fellow's shoulder.

Shepard's left arm dropped limply. He dashed toward the door and forced his way past, firing wildly at such close range that it almost burst the gallant policeman's ear drums.

Up the ladder he scurried like a wild animal, firing as he climbed.

Burke was right behind him.

Shepard ran for the fire-escape. Burke was after him. Each man was wasting bullets. But as Shepard reached the edge of the roof Burke took the most deliberate aim of his life, and sent a bullet into the villain's breast.

Shepard gasped, his hands went up, and he toppled over the cornice to the back yard below.

He died as he had lived, with a curse on his lip, murder in his heart, and battling like a beast!

CHAPTER XV

THE FINISH

Burke rushed down the dilapidated steps once more to the room where Lorna had undergone her bitter punishment. Already three bluecoats had entered in time to capture the frantic old woman, while they worked to bring the miserable girl back to consciousness.

"She's coming around all right, Burke," said the sergeant. "Help me carry her downstairs."

"I'll do that myself," quoth Bobbie, feeling that the privilege of restoring her to Mary had been rightfully earned. He picked her up and tenderly lifted her from the couch where she had been placed by the sergeant. Down the stairs they went with their prisoner, while Patrolman White descended from the roof with his captive, whose hands had been shackled behind his back.

The house had the appearance of a cheap lodging place, and the dirty carpet of the hall showed hard usage. As they reached the lower floor Bobbie noticed Captain Sawyer rummaging through an imitation mahogany desk in the converted parlor, a room furnished much after the fashion of the bedroom of Madame Blanche in the house uptown.

"What sort of place is it? A headquarters for the gang?" asked Bobbie, as he hesitated with Lorna in his arms.

"No, just the same kind of joint we've raided so many times, and we've got hundreds more to raid," answered Sawyer. "I've found the receipts for the rent here, and they've been paying about five times what it is worth. The man who owns this house is your friend Trubus. This links him up once more. There's a lot of information in this desk. But hurry with the girl, Bobbie, for her sister is nearly wild."

As Burke marched down the steps, carrying the rescued one, a big crowd of jostling spectators raised a howl of "bravos" for the gallant bluecoat. The nature of this evil establishment was well enough known in the neighborhood, but people of that part of town knew well enough to keep their information from the police, for the integrity of their own skins.

Mary had been kept inside the automobile with difficulty; now she screamed with joy and sprang from the step to the street. Up the stone stairs she rushed, throwing her arms about Lorna, who greeted her with a wan smile; she had strength for no more evidence of recognition.

"Here, chief," said the chauffeur of the hired car to Burke, "I always have this handy in my machine. Give the lady a drink—it'll help her."

He had drawn forth a brandy flask, and Burke quickly unscrewed the cup-cap, to pour out a libation.

"Oh, no!" moaned Lorna, objecting weakly, but Burke forced it between her teeth. The burning liquid roused her energies and, with Mary's assistance, she was able to sit up in the rear of the auto.

"Take another, lady," volunteered the chauffeur. "It'll do you good."

"Never. I've tasted the last liquor that shall ever pass my lips," said Lorna. "Oh, Mary, what a horrible lesson I've learned!"

Her sister comforted her, and turned toward Burke pleadingly.

"Can I take her home, Bob? You know how anxious father is?"

Captain Sawyer had come to the side of the automobile. He nodded.

"Yes, Miss Barton, the chauffeur will take her right up to your house. Give her some medical attention at once, and be ready to come back with her to the station house as soon as I send for you. I'm going to get the ringleader of this gang in my net before the day is through. So your sister should be here if she is strong enough to press the first complaint. I'll attend to the others, with the Federal Government and those phonograph records back of me! Hurry up, now."

He turned to his sergeant.

"Put these prisoners in the other automobile and call out the men to clear this mob away from the streets. Keep the house watched by one man outside and one in the rear. We don't know what might be done to destroy some of this evidence."

The automobile containing the two girls started on the glad homeward journey at the Captain's signal. Bobbie waved his hat and the happy tears coursed down his face.

"Well, Captain, I've got to face a serious investigation now," he said to his superior as they went up the steps once more.

"What is it?" exclaimed Sawyer in surprise, "You'll be a medal of honor man, my boy."

"I've killed a man."

"You have! Well, tell me about your end of the raid. All this has happened so quickly that we must get the report ready right here on the spot, in order to have it exact."

"This man Shepard, who seems to be the professional whipper of this gang, as well as a procurer, fought me with a magazine revolver. I ran him up to the roof, and I had to shoot him or be killed myself. That means a trial, I know. You'll find his body back of the house, for he fell off the roof at the end."

"Self-defense and carrying out the law will cover you, my boy. Don't worry about that. This city has been kept terror-stricken by these gangsters long enough, because honest citizens have been compelled by a ward politician's law to go without weapons of defense. A man is not allowed to have a revolver in his own home without paying ten dollars a year as a license fee. But a crook can carry an arsenal; I've always had a sneaking opinion that there were two sides to the reasons for that law. Then the city officials have given the public the idea that the police were brutes, and have reprimanded us for using force with these murderers and robbers. Force is the only thing that will tame these beasts of the jungle. You can't do it with kisses and boxes of candy!"

Burke was rubbing his left forearm.

"By Jingo! I believe I hurt myself."

He rolled up his sleeve, and saw a furrow of red in his muscular forearm. It was bleeding, but as he wiped it with his handkerchief he was relieved to find that it was a mere flesh wound.

"If Shepard had hit the right instead of the left—I would have been left in the discard," he said, with grim humor. "Can you help me tie it up for now. This means another scolding from Doctor MacFarland, I suppose."

"It means that you've more evidence of the need for putting a tiger out of danger!"

The coroner was called, and the statements of the policemen were made. The Captain, with Burke and several men, deployed through the back yard to the other house, leaving the grewsome duty of removing the body to the coroner. The two waiting automobiles on the rear street were crowded with policemen, as Sawyer ordered the chauffeur to drive speedily to the headquarters of the Purity League.

"We must clean out that hole, as we did this one!" muttered Sawyer. "You go for Trubus, Burke, with one of the men, while I will take the rest and close in on their 'Mercantile' office downstairs. We'll put that slave market out of business in three minutes."

They were soon on Fifth Avenue. The elevators carried the policemen up to the third floor, and they sprang into the offices of the "Mercantile Association" with little ado.

The small, wan man who sat at the desk was just in the act of sniffing a cheering potion of cocaine as the head of Captain Sawyer appeared through the door. With a quick movement the lookout pressed two buttons. One of them resulted in a metallic click in the door of the strong iron grating. The other rang a warning bell inside the private office of John Clemm.

Sawyer pushed and shoved at the grilled barrier, but it was safely locked with a strong, secret bolt.

"Open this, or I'll shoot!" exclaimed the irate Captain.

"You can't get in there. We're a lawful business concern," replied the little man, squirming toward the door which led to the big waiting room. "Where's your search warrant. I know the law, and you police can't fool me."

"This is my search warrant!" exclaimed Sawyer, as he sent a bullet crashing into the wall, purposely aiming a foot above the lookout's head. "Quick, open this door. The next shot won't miss!"

There was a sound of overturned chairs and cries of alarm inside the door. The little man felt that he had sounded his warning and lived up to his duty. Had he completed that sniffing of the "koke," he would doubtless have been stimulated to enough pseudo-courage to face the entire Police Department single-handed—as long as the thrill of the drug lasted. A majority of the desperate deeds performed by the criminals in New York, so medical examinations have proved, are carried on under the stimulus of this fearful poison, which can be obtained with comparative ease throughout the city.

But the lookout was deprived of his drug. He even endeavored to take a sniff as the captain and his men shoved and shook the iron work of the grating.

"Drop it!" cried Sawyer, pulling the trigger again and burying another bullet in the plaster.

"Oh, oh! Don't shoot!" cried the lookout weakly. He trembled as he advanced to the grating and removed the emergency bolt.

"Grab him!" cried Sawyer to one of his men. "Come with me, fellows." He rushed into the waiting room. There consternation reigned. Fully a dozen pensioners of the "system" of traffic in souls were struggling to escape through the barred windows in the rear. These bars had been placed as they were to resist the invaders from the outside. John Clemm's system of defense was extremely ingenious. In time of trouble he had not deemed the inmates of the middle room worth protecting—his purpose was to exclude with the iron grating and the barred windows the possible entry of raiders.

Three revolvers were on the floor. Their owners had wisely discarded them to avoid the penalty of the concealed weapon law, for they had realized that they were trapped.

"Open that door!" cried Sawyer, who had learned the arrangement of the rooms from Burke's description.

Two men pushed at the door, which was securely locked. They finally caught up the nearest church pew, and, using it as a battering ram, they succeeded in smashing the heavy oaken panels. The door had been barricaded with a cross bar. As they cautiously peered in through the forced opening they saw the room empty and the window open.

"He's escaped!" exclaimed Sawyer.

Just then a call from the outer vestibule reached his ears.

"I've caught the go-between, Captain. Here's Mr. John Clemm, the executive genius of this establishment," sung out Burke, who was standing inside the door with the rueful fat man wearing the handcuffs.

"Where did you get him, Burke?"

"He tried to make a quiet getaway through the rescue department of the Purity League," answered Officer 4434. "I nabbed him as he came up the fire-escape from this floor."

"Where is Trubus?"

"He has gone home, so one of the stenographers tells me."

"Then we will get him, too. Hurry now. White, I leave you in charge of this place. Send for the wagon and take these men over to our station house. Get every bit of paper and the records. We had better look around in that private office first before we go after Trubus."

They finished the demolition of the door and entered.

"What's this arrangement?" queried Sawyer, puzzled, as he looked at the automatic pencil box.

"That is an arrangement by which this fellow Clemm has been making duplicates of all his transactions in his own writing," explained Burke. "You see this Trubus has trusted no one. He has a definite record of every deal spread out before him by the other pencil on the machine upstairs, just as this go-between writes it out. Then here is the dictagraph, under the desk."

Burke pointed out the small transmitting disc to the surprised captain.

"Well, this man learned a lot from the detectives and applied it to his trade very scientifically, didn't he?"

"Yes, the records we have on the phonograph show that every word which passed in this room was received upstairs by Trubus. No one but Clemm knew of his connection or ownership of the establishment. Yet Trubus, all the time that he was posing as the guardian angel of virtue, has been familiar with the work of every procurer and every purchaser; it's a wonderful system. If he had spent as much energy on doing the charitable work that he pretended to do, think of how much misery and sickness he could have cured."

"Well, Burke, it's the same game that a lot of politicians on the East Side do. They own big interests and the gambling privileges in the saloons, and they get their graft from the gangsters. Then about twice a year they give a picnic for the mothers and babies of the drunkards who patronize their saloons. They send a ticket for a bucket of coal or a pair of shoes to the parents of young girls who work for the gangsters and bring the profits of shame back tenfold on the investment to these same politicians. They will spend a hundred dollars on charity and the newspapers will run columns about it. But the poor devils who cheer them and vote for them don't realize that every dollar of graft comes, not out of the pockets of property owners and employers, but from reduced wages, increased rents, and expensive, rotten food. Trubus would have been a great Alderman or State Senator: he wasted his talents on religion."

Burke turned to the door.

"Shall I go up to his house, Captain? I'd like to be in at the finish of this whole fight."

"You bet you can," said Sawyer. "It's now nearly six o'clock, and we will jump into the machine and get up there before he can get out to supper. The men will take care of these prisoners."

After a few skillful orders, Sawyer led the way downstairs. They were soon speeding up to the Riverside Drive residence of the philanthropist, Sawyer and Burke enjoying the machine to themselves.

"This is a joy ride that will not be so joyful for one man on the return trip, Burke!" exclaimed Sawyer, as he took off his cap to mop the perspiration from his brow. He had been through a strenuous afternoon and was beginning to feel the strain.

"How shall we approach his house?" asked Burke.

"You get out of the machine and go to the door. There's no need of alarming his family. Just tell the servant who answers the door that you want to speak to the boss—say that there's been a robbery down at his office, and you want to speak to him privately. Tell the servant not to let the other members of the family know about it, as it would worry them."

"That's a good idea, Captain. I understand that his wife and daughter are very fine women. It will save a terrible scene. What a shame to make them suffer like this!"

"Yes, Burke. If these scoundrels only realized that their work always made some good woman suffer—sometimes a hundred. Think of the women that this villain has made to suffer, body and soul. Think of the mothers' hearts he has broken while posing with his charity and his Bible! All that wickedness is to be punished on his own wife and his own daughter. I tell you, there's something in life which brings back the sins of the fathers, all right, upon their children. The Good Book certainly tells it right."

The auto was stopped before the handsome residence of the Purity League's leader. It seemed a bitter tangle of Fate that in these beautiful surroundings, with the broad blue Hudson River a few hundred yards away, the green of the park trees, the happy throng of pedestrians strolling and chatting along the promenade of the Drive, it should be Burke's duty to drag to punishment as foul a scoundrel as ever drew the breath of the beautiful spring air. The sun was setting in the heights of Jersey, across the Hudson, and the golden light tinted the carved stone doorway of Trubus's home, making Burke feel as though he were acting in some stage drama, rather than real life. The spotlight of Old Sol was on him as he rang the bell by the entry.

"Is Mr. Trubus home?" asked Burke of the portly butler who answered the summons.

"Hi don't know, sir," responded the servant, in a conventional monotone. "What nyme, sir?"

"Just tell him that it is a policeman. His office has been robbed, and we want to get some particulars about it."

"Well, sir, he's dressing for dinner, sir. You'll 'ave to wyte, sir. Hi wouldn't dare disturb 'im now, sir."

"You had better dare. This is very important to him. But don't mention it to anyone else, for it would worry his wife and daughter."

As Burke was speaking, a big fashionable car drew up behind the one in which Captain Sawyer sat, awaiting developments. A young man, wearing a light overcoat, whose open fold displayed a dinner coat, descended and approached the door.

"What's the trouble here?" he curtly inquired.

"None of your business," snapped Burke, who recognized the fiancé, Ralph Gresham.

"Don't you sauce me—I'll find out myself."

The butler bowed as Gresham approached.

"Come in, sir. Miss Trubus is hexpecting you, sir. This person is wyting to see Mr. Trubus, sir."

Gresham, with an angry look at the calm policeman, went inside.

The door shut. Burke for a minute regretted that he had not insisted on admission. It might have been possible for Trubus to have received some sort of warning. The "best-laid plans of mice and men" had one bad habit, as Burke recollected, just at the moment when success was apparently within grasp.

But the door opened again. The smug countenance, the neatly brushed "mutton-chops," the immaculate dinner coat of William Trubus appeared, and Bobbie looked up into the angry glint of the gentleman's black eyes.

"What do you mean by annoying me here? Why didn't you telephone me?" began the owner of the mansion. "I am just going out to dinner."

He looked sharply at Burke, vaguely remembering the face of the young officer. Bobbie quietly stepped to his side and caught the knob of the big door, shutting it softly behind Trubus.

"Why, you...."

Before he could finish Burke had deftly clipped one handcuff on the right wrist of the man and with an unexpected movement pinioned the other, snapping the manacle as he did so.

"Outrageous!" exclaimed the astounded Trubus. But Burke was dragging him rapidly into the car.

"If you don't want your wife to know about this, get in quickly," commanded Sawyer sharply.

Trubus began to expostulate, but his thick lips quivered with emotion.

"Down to the station house, quick!" ordered the captain to the chauffeur. "No speed limit."

"I'll have you discharged from the force for this, you scoundrel!" Trubus finally found words to say. "Where is your warrant for my arrest? What is your charge?"

Sawyer did not answer.

As they reached a subway station he called out to the driver:

"Stop a minute. Now, Burke, you had better go uptown and get the witness; hurry right down, for I want to end this matter to-night."

Bobbie dismounted, while Trubus stormed in vain. As the car sped onward he saw the president of the Purity League indulging in language quite alien to the Scriptural quotations which were his usual stock in discourse. Captain Sawyer was puffing a cigar and watching the throng on the sidewalks as though he were stone deaf.

Burke hurried to the Barton home. There he found a scene of joy which beggared description. Lorna had recovered and was strong enough to run to greet him.

"Oh, Mr. Burke, can you ever forgive me for my silliness and ugly words?" she began, as Mary caught the officer's hand with a welcome clasp.

"There, there, Miss Lorna, I've nothing to forgive. I'm so happy that you have come out safe and sound from the dangers of these men," answered Burke. "We have trapped the gang, even up to Trubus, and, if you are strong enough to go down to the station, we will have him sent with the rest of his crew to the Tombs to await trial."

Old Barton reached for Burke's hand.

"My boy, you have been more than a friend to me on this terrible yet wonderful day. You could have done no more if you had been my own son."

The excitement and his own tense nerves drove Bobbie to a speech which he had been pondering and hesitating to make for several weeks. He blurted it out now, intensely surprised at his own temerity.

"Your own son, Mr. Barton.... Oh, how I wish I were.... And I hope that I may be some day, if you and some one else are willing ... some day when I have saved enough to provide the right sort of a home."

He hesitated, and Lorna stepped back. Mary held out her hands, and her eyes glowed with that glorious dilation which only comes once in a life-time to one woman's glance for only one man's answering look.

She held out her hands as she approached him.

"Oh, Bob ... as though you had to ask!" was all she said, as the strong arms caught her in their first embrace. Her face was wet with tears as Bob drew back from their first kiss.

John Barton was wiping his eyes as Burke looked at him in happy bewilderment at this curious turn to his fortune.

"My boy, Bob," began the old man softly, "would you take the responsibility of a wife, earning no more money than a policeman can?"

Bob nodded. "I'd do it and give up everything in the world to make her happy if it were enough to satisfy her," he asserted.

Barton lifted up a letter which had been lying on the table beside him. He smiled as he read from it:

"DEAR MR. BARTON:

"The patents have gone through in great shape and they are so basic that no one can fight you on them. The Gresham Company has offered me, as your attorney, fifty thousand dollars as an advance royalty, and a contract for your salary as superintendent for their manufacture. We can get even more. It may interest you to know that your friend on the police force won't have to worry about a raise in salary. I have been working on his case with a lawyer in Decatur, Illinois. His uncle is willing to make a payment of twenty-four thousand dollars to prevent being prosecuted for misappropriation of funds on that estate. I will see you...."

Barton dropped the letter to his lap.

"Now, how does that news strike you?"

"I can't believe it real," gasped Burke, rubbing his forehead. "But I am more glad for you than for myself. You will have an immense fortune, won't you?"

Smiling into the faces of the two radiant girls, Old Barton drew Lorna to his side and, reaching forward, tugged at the hand of Mary.

"In my two dear girls, safe and happy, I have a greater wealth for my old age than the National City Bank could pay me, Burke. Lorna has told me of her experience and her escape when all escape seemed hopeless. She has learned that the sensual pleasures of one side of New York's glittering life are dross and death. In the books and silly plays she has read and seen it was pictured as being all song and jollity. Now she knows how sordid and bitter is the draught which can only end, like all poison, in one thing. God bless you, my boy, and you, my girls!"

Bobbie shook the old man's hand, and then remembered the unpleasant duty still before him.

"We must get down town as soon as possible," syd he. "Come, won't you go with us, Mary?"

The two girls put on their hats and together they traveled to the distant police station as rapidly as possible. It was a bitter ordeal for Lorna, whose strength was nearly exhausted. The welts on her shoulders from Shepard's whip brought the tears to her eyes. As they reached the station house the girl became faint. The matron and Mary had to chafe her hands and apply other homely remedies to keep her up for the task of identifying the woman who had been captured.

"Now, Burke," began Sawyer, "I have been saving Trubus for a surprise. He has been locked up in my private office, and still doesn't know exactly how we have caught him. I've broken the letter of the rules by forbidding him to telephone anyone until you came. I guess it is important enough, in view of our discovery, for me to have done this—he can call up his lawyer as soon as we have confronted him with Clemm and this young girl. Bring me the phonograph records."

They went into his private office, where White was guarding Trubus.

"How much longer am I to be subject to these Russian police methods?" demanded Trubus, with an oath.

"Quiet, now, Mr. Purity League," said Sawyer, "we are going to have ladies present. You will soon be allowed to talk all you want. But I warn you in advance that everything you say will be used as evidence against you."

"Against me—me, the leading charity worker of our city!" snorted Trubus, but he watched the door uneasily.

"Bring in the young ladies, Burke," directed Captain Sawyer.

Bobbie returned with Mary and Lorna. Trubus started perceptibly as he observed the new telephone girl whom his wife had induced him to employ that day.

Sawyer nodded again to Burke.

"Now the go-between." He turned to Mary. "Do you know this man, Miss Barton?"

The name had a strangely familiar sound to Trubus. He wondered uneasily.

"He is William Trubus, president of the Purity League. I worked for him to-day."

"Do you recognize this man?" was queried, as Clemm shuffled forward, with the assistance of Burke's sturdy push.

"This is the one who was embracing the other telephone girl. But he did not stay there long. I never saw him before that, to my recollection."

"What do you know about this man, Officer 4434?" asked the captain. Clemm fumbled with his handcuffs, looking down in a sheepish way to avoid the malevolent looks of Trubus.

"He is known as John Clemm, although we have found a police record of him under a dozen different aliases. He formerly ran a gambling house, and at different times has been involved in bunco game and wire-tapping tricks. He is one of the cleverest crooks in New York. In the present case he has been the go-between for this man Trubus, who, posing as a reformer to cover his activities, has kept in touch with the work of the Vice Trust, managed by Clemm. They had a dictagraph and a mechanical pencil register which connected Trubus's office with Clemm's."

"It's a lie!" shouted Trubus, furiously. "Some of these degraded criminals are drawing my famous and honored name into this case to protect themselves. It is a police scheme for notoriety."

"You'll get the notoriety," retorted Sawyer. "There is a young man who is taking notes for the biggest paper in New York. He has verified every detail. They'll have extras on the streets in fifteen minutes, for this is the biggest story in years. You are cornered at last, Trubus. Send in the rest of those people arrested in that house owned by Trubus." The woman was brought in with the others of the gang who had been apprehended in the old house.

The pretended philanthropist was cornered at last.

"Now, Mr. Trubus, this woman rented from you and paid a very high rental. The man Shepard was killed in resisting arrest. We have rounded up Baxter,

Craig, Madame Blanche and a dozen others of your employees. Have you anything to say?"

Trubus whirled around and would have struck Clemm had not White intervened.

"You squealer! You've betrayed me!"

"No, I didn't!" cried Clemm, shrinking back. "I swear I didn't!"

Sawyer reached for the phonograph records and held them up with a laconic smile.

"There's no use in accusing anyone else, Trubus. You're your own worst enemy, for these records, with your own dictagraph as the chief assistant prosecutor, have trapped you."

Trubus raised his hands in terror and his iron nerve gave way completely.

"Oh, my God!" he cried. "What will my wife and daughter think?"

"You should have figured that out when you started all this," retorted Sawyer. "Take them into the cells, and we'll have them arraigned at Night Court. Make out the full reports now, men."

The prisoners were led out.

Trubus turned and begged with Sawyer for a little time.

"Let me tell my wife," he pleaded. "I don't want any one else to do it."

"You stay just where you are, until I am through with you. You're getting war methods now, Trubus—after waging war from ambush for all this time. Burke, you had better have the young ladies taken home. Go up with them. Use the automobile outside. You can have the evening off as soon as we get through the arraignment at court."

It took an hour before the first charges could be brought to the Magistrate, through whose hands all cases must first be carried. The sisters decided to stay and end their first ordeal with what testimony was desired. This was sufficient for the starting of the wheels of justice. Trubus had called up his lawyer, who was on hand with the usual objections and instructions. But he was held over until the day court, without bail.

"Only let me go home, and break the news to my wife and daughter," begged the subdued man. "Oh, I beg that one privilege."

The judge looked at Captain Sawyer, who nodded.

"I will send a couple of men up with him, your honor. I understand his wife is a very estimable lady. It will be a bitter blow to her."

"All right. You will have to go in the custody of the police. But I will not release you on bail."

Bobbie and the girls had already sped on their way to the happy Barton home. Trubus, under the watchful eyes of two policemen and with his lawyer, lost no time in returning to his mansion.

As he rang the bell the butler hurried to the door in a frightened manner.

"It can't be true, sir, wot the pypers say, can it?" he gasped. But Trubus forced his way past, followed by the attorney and his two guards.

In the beautiful drawing-room he saw two maids leaning over the Oriental couch. They were trying to quiet his daughter.

"Why, Sylvia, my child," he cried.

"Oh, oh!" exclaimed the girl, forcing herself free from the restraining hands of the servants. She laughed shrilly as she staggered toward her father. Her eyes were wide and staring with the light of madness. "Here's father! Dear father!"

Trubus paled, but caught her in his arms.

"My poor dear," he began.

"Oh, look, father, what it says in the papers. We missed you—ha, ha!—and the newsboys sold us this on the street. Look, father, there's your picture. He, he! And Ralph bought it and brought it to me."

She staggered and sank half-drooping in his arms. Her head rolled back and her eyes stared wildly at the ceiling. Her mad laughter rang out shrilly, piercing the ears of her miserable father. The two policemen and the lawyer watched the uncanny scene.

"Ha, ha! Ralph read it, and he's gone. He wouldn't marry me now, he said,—ha, ha! Father! Who cares? Oh, it's so funny!" She broke from her father's hold and ran into the big dining room, pursued by the sobbing maids.

"She's gone crazy as a loon," whispered one of the policemen to the other.

"Where is my wife?" timidly asked Trubus, as he supported himself with one hand on a table near the door. The frightened butler, with choleric red face, pointed upward.

Trubus drew himself up and started for the broad stairway.

Just then a revolver shot smote the ears of the excited men. It came from above.

"Great God!" uttered Trubus, clasping his hand to his heart. He ran for the stairs, followed by the two patrolmen, while the lawyer sank weakly into a chair and buried his face in his hands. He guessed only too well what had happened.

The policemen were slower than the panic-stricken Trubus.

They found him in his magnificent boudoir, kneeling and sobbing by the side of his dead wife; a revolver had fallen to the floor from her limp hand. It was still smoking. The exquisite lace coverlet was even now drinking up the red stains, and the bluecoats stopped at the doorway, dropping their heads as they instinctively doffed their caps.

Gruff Roundsman Murphy crossed himself, while White wiped his eyes with the back of his hand. He remembered a verse from the old days when he went to Sunday-school in the Jersey town where he was born.

"'Vengeance is mine,' saith the Lord."

The blossoms of late May were tinting the greensward beneath the trees of Central Park as Bobbie Burke and Mary strolled along one of the winding paths. They had just walked up the Avenue from their last shopping expedition.

"I hated to bid the boys at the station house good-bye this afternoon, Mary. Yet after to-night we'll be away from New York for a wonderful month in the country. And then no more police duty, is there?"

"No, Bob. You and father will be the busiest partners in New York and you will have to report for duty at our new little apartment every evening before six. I'm so glad that you can leave all those dangers, and gladder still because of my own selfish gratifications. After to-night."

"Well, I'm scared of to-night more than I was of that police parade on May Day, with all that fuss about the medal. Here I've got to face a minister, and you know that's not as easy as it seems."

They reached the new home which the advance royalties for old Barton's days of realization had made possible. It was a handsome apartment on Central Park West, and the weeks of preparation had turned it into a wonderful bower for this night of nights.

"Look, Mary," cried Lorna, as they came in. "Here are two more presents. One must weigh a ton and the other is in this funny old bandbox."

They opened the big bundle first; it was a silver service of elaborate, ornate design. It had cost hundreds of dollars.

On a long paper Bobbie saw the names of a hundred men, all familiar and memory-stirring. The list was headed with the simple dedication in the full, round hand which Burke recognized as that of Captain Sawyer:

"To the Prince of all the Rookies and his Princess, from his brother cops. God bless you, Bobbie Burke, and Mrs. Bobbie."

Ex-officer 4434 Burke blinked and hugged his happy fiancée delightedly.

"What's in that old bandbox, Bob?" asked Lorna. "It's marked 'Glass—Handle with care.' I wonder how it ever held together. Some country fellow left it at the door this afternoon, but wouldn't come in."

They opened it, and Mary gasped.

"Why, look at the flowers!"

The box seemed full of old-fashioned country blossoms, as Mary dipped her hand into it. Then she deftly reached to the bottom of the big bandbox and lifted its contents. Wrapped in a sheathing of oiled tissue paper was a monstrous cake, layer on layer, like a Chinese pagoda. It was covered with that rustic triumph of multi-colored icing which only grandmothers seem able to compound in these degenerate days of machine-made pastry of the city bakeries.

A wedding ring of yellow icing was molded in the center, while on either side were red candy hearts, joined by whirly sugar streamers of pink and blue.

A card pinned in the center said:

"From Henrietta and Joe."

"That's all we needed," said Mary with a sob in her happy voice, "to make our wedding supper end right. Wasn't it, Officer 4434?"

THE END

Milton Keynes UK
Ingram Content Group UK Ltd.
UKHW010850010724
444982UK00005B/516